One Man's Quest for Forgiveness Amid Pursuit
of Restoration to His Family and His God

A Pastor's Story

Tim Pinkerton

A Pastor's Story
Copyright © 2024 by Tim Pinkerton. All rights reserved.

No part of this book may be used or reproduced in any manner whatsoever without written permission, except in the case of brief quotations embodied in critical articles and reviews. For more information, e-mail all inquiries to info@mindstirmedia.com.

Published by MindStir Media, LLC45 Lafayette Rd | Suite 181| North Hampton, NH 03862 | USA
1.800.767.0531 | www.mindstirmedia.com

Printed in the United States of America.
ISBN-13: 978-1-963844-34-4

ACKNOWLEDGEMENTS

To my pastor, Kevin Sartin: Your advice and sage wisdom were invaluable during the progression of this project. From the bottom of my heart, I say "Thank you" and may God continue to bless your pastoral ministry.

To my dear friend, Tot Cargile: Your follow-along in the reading and proofing of the text was pivotal in getting the manuscript to completion. My sincerest thanks for your effort and hours spent and for your gentle nudges to "keep on keeping on."

To my wife, Dena: Your willingness to give me the time and space needed to write this story helped me mark a long-held dream off my bucket list. Thank you for your patience. I love you with all my heart.

Lastly, to my Lord and Savior Jesus Christ in Whom my faith rests: May your name be uplifted in the following pages. To You be honor and glory forever!

"When young, you're shocked by the number of people who turn out to have feet of clay. Older, you're surprised by the number of people who don't."

Malcom Forbes

Feet of clay. It's a word picture that refers to the unfortunate truth that the imperfections and shortcomings of those whom we place on pedestals because of the positions they hold and the work that they do tend to show up at the most inopportune times. It's probably safe to say that nearly all of us have been disappointed at some time in our lives by someone we looked up to. Children experience such disappointments with their parents. Fans with sports heroes and celebrities. Employees with supervisors, managers, and corporate officers. And (maybe most unfortunately of all), church members with pastors and other church leaders. When the ones whose moral compasses are always supposed to point to true north reveal their feet of clay, the resulting devastation can be especially far-reaching.

As someone who has spent the past two decades serving as the pastor of smaller-membership churches, I feel a sense of kinship with the main character in my friend Tim Pinkerton's story that you now hold in your hands. Trying to minister to others while wrestling with one's own fallen humanity can be a daunting task, to say the least. Pastors have faults and flaws, too. And so, on one level, this is a story about imperfect humanity. It's a story about dealing with hardship and difficulty. It's a story about recovering from failure and loss. But at its core, I would say that this is a story about God's grace. It's a story about God's faithfulness and His provision and His ability to use imperfect people to accomplish His perfect purposes. And because all of us fail and fall and need God's grace, I think this is a story that has the potential to resonate with people from all different walks of life. God is gracious, and we all need to be reminded of that often.

And though pastoral ministry does have its share of challenges, those challenges are balanced by some incredible rewards. Some of the deepest joys that I've experienced in vocational ministry have come in the form of relationships cultivated with those I've had the privilege of serving. As I have gotten to know Tim over the past nearly 12 years that I have served as the pastor of First Baptist Church in Nashville, Arkansas, I have enjoyed his friendship and benefitted from his encouragement, and I have greatly appreciated the opportunity to watch him persevere in his journey of sharing this story with the world. I hope that you enjoy it as much as I did the first time that I read it.

Kevin Sartin
Pastor, First Baptist Nashville, AR

PROLOGUE

Saturday, June 9, 2012, 10:23 A.M.

Matt McDonald grabbed the bottle of water from the cup holder and gulped down what was left in it. He tossed it in the seat and flipped the a/c setting to high level. It was unseasonably hot for late spring, and he didn't handle heat well. But he would today. Because this day was special. It was daddy and daughter day out. But before the fun could begin, he faced a challenge. And that challenge was just moments away.

In the passenger seat, dressed in shorts, a red pullover top, and baby blue flip flops, his eight-year-old daughter Angela sat engrossed in the wacky antics of <u>Amelia Bedelia</u>. From the grin on her face, she was finding the story as funny now as she had all the other times she'd read it. He noticed she was nearing the end of the book. And after the next sharp curve, Miller Lake would appear.

Tell her Matt....TOMORROW...When you go by the lake...She's mature for her age....She'll understand....You shouldn't have promised her we'd go back!

Why did Carol have to be so scared of everything, especially water? Now, as his wife's words of the previous evening ricocheted through his head, his chest throbbed with an ache that was more punishing than painful.

*But, I did promise her....She won't understand.....
We won't be in the water long....I'll be right beside her
every second.*

His rebuttal had been in vain. Seeing Carol's anguish quickly
escalate to tears, he had finally caved. Now, his bad daddy moment
was at hand.

Angela closed the book with a loud **POP!** and dropped it in the
seat next to her. She giggled and sized up the book's ditzy simpleton.

"That girl is SOOOO silly!" she said. "How can anybody be that
silly, Daddy?"

Matt reached over and patted the red bow nestled on top of her
black curls. "I don't know, Angel," he said, taking her tiny hand in
his and smiling down at her.

He released her hand and placed his palm back on the steering
wheel. Safely through the bend, he accelerated and a half-mile
farther, the tree line to his right gave way to an expanse of silvery,
shimmering water stretching far and wide to the west.

Tell her Matt.....TOMORROW....When you go by the lake.

His words spilled forth rapidly. "We sure had fun swimming the
other day, didn't we?"

"Uh-huh!" Angela said. "Except when I got water up my nose.
That hurt."

Hurt? It was the perfect lead-in. But before he could grab the
opportunity, Angela continued, her voice raised and excited.

"Can we go see Daisy?"

He hadn't expected this. As his brain struggled for how to
answer her, an image of a small, feathered creature filled his head. It
had been just two weeks ago, on a casual outing at the picnic area just
ahead, while standing near the end of the wooden pier at Arrowhead
Point, that Angela had spied a mallard hen.

"Mommy! Daddy! Look!" she had yelled, pointing in the direction of an islet some thirty feet to the pier's right. "It's a goose!"

Camouflaged by her dull brown plumage, the bird had been barely visible except for the erratic twitches of her head. Peeking out from under her dappled feathers were the outer rims of cream-colored and pale blue eggs.

"That's not a goose, Angel," Matt had said, smiling. "That's a momma duck on her nest. She's gonna have babies. See her eggs?"

"I see four. She's gonna have four babies, Mommy."

Carol had grinned and drawn her daughter close. "There may be some eggs we can't see, Angel. So, she may have more than four. That'll be a big family, won't it?"

"That's bigger than Robin's family!" Angela had replied, referring to the mother robin that had just raised three young in their backyard silver maple. "A lot bigger!"

Before leaving, Angela had turned and circled her mouth with both hands. "Bye, Daisy!" she had yelled. Unfazed by the sound of her new name, the mother duck had remained silent.

Now, Angela's plea squeezed his heart like a vice. "Can we Daddy? Please? I bet she has babies."

It can't hurt anything, Matt told himself. *I'll hold her hand the whole time. And it'll be our secret. Her mother will never have to know.*

Carol's words echoed inside his head. ***I don't want her near water ever again! Not even close to it! Promise me you'll tell her, Matt!***

It had been only hours since he had made that promise. Now, he was about to break it. His insides tightened. Still, he couldn't find it in his heart to tell his Angel no. After all, what would it hurt?

"I don't see why not," Matt replied, guilt surging through him.

Angela bounced with eagerness. "Thank you, Daddy!"

Matt's brow furrowed. "You know, Angel, the eggs may not have hatched yet. Momma ducks sit on them for a long time. "

It was a ploy. Would it change her mind and buy him some time?

Angela stared out the window at the lake water shining in the bright sunlight. "I still wanna go see her," she said.

"Okay, Angel," Matt said as another pang of guilt sliced through him.

South Shore Landing was deserted except for a dark blue beat-up Ford Pickup. Matt parked three spaces away from it and cut the engine. He raised the console and gestured for Angela to slide toward him. She eased across to cuddle against him.

"I need you to hold my hand the whole time, Angel," Matt whispered in her ear. "Don't let go of it, okay?"

She nodded and the two of them climbed out of the truck. As they descended the concrete pathway, Matt detected movement in the playground just past the open pavilion. Scurrying around in the network of yellow crawl tubes, orange tunnel slides, and green muscle bars were two young boys, both lanky with blond hair. They wore athletic tops and dark shorts and were so drenched in sweat they looked like they had just emerged from the swimming area nearby. On a bench near them sat a heavy-set, middle-aged woman wearing a white tank top and striped shorts that reached past her knees. Her reddish-blond hair was pushed back from her forehead by a dark blue visor.

Be friendly but keep moving, Matt told himself. *Find Daisy and get back on the road.*

"Hello," he yelled, waving his free hand.

"Hi," the woman replied. "Nice day to be outside, huh?"

"Ya'll be careful," Matt said firmly. "Heat like this is dangerous. Hope you're drinkin' plenty of water."

"We'll be fine," she said assuredly. "Won't be long til' we head down to the water and take a dip."

Matt raised his thumb in approval. "Maybe we'll see you on our way back."

He renewed his grip on Angela's hand as they passed over a tree-covered knoll and descended to the pier a hundred yards away. Stepping up on the splintered planks, the two paused to catch their breath. Expectantly, they walked to the end of the rude structure.

The nest was empty and lonely-looking. Down feathers lay randomly about, swaying in a faint breeze. Broken eggshells lay clustered inside the bowl of the nest, a mute testament to the life that had recently burst forth. But Daisy and her babies were nowhere to be seen.

"She's gone, Daddy. Did she take her babies away?"

"I'm not sure, Angel. Let's go see if they're around on the other side of the point."

Again, he squeezed her hand as they made their way back to shore. As they stepped off the pier, an alarming interruption.

HELP!

The scream—bone chilling and noxious—pierced the thick heavy air like a knife. Then, it repeated, louder and more acute than before.

PLEASE! SOMEBODY HELP US!

Matt's eyes widened. *The woman and her sons. They're in trouble. And there's nobody else here.*

He stared down at Angela. Her eyes were filled with fear and confusion. She released his hand and burrowed into his side, circling his waist with both arms.

"I'm scared, Daddy," she whimpered. "Can we go?"

Staring in the direction of the screams, Matt's mind spun in circles as he processed the possibilities. Was there blood? Or even death? Was it an attacker?

He had to help. But as he stood rooted to the ground, a chilling reality hit him.

I can't take her with me!

He spotted a large boulder near the base of a pine tree a safe distance from the water's edge. Hurriedly, he pulled Angela toward it. Kneeling to a squatting position, he circled both of her hands with his, then leaned forward and kissed her forehead.

"I need you to sit here 'til I get back, Angel. Those people up there are in trouble, and they need my help." He framed her tear-moistened cheeks in his hands. "You can't go with me. You might get hurt."

The Lord will protect her, he assured himself. *Have faith!*

"Promise me you won't move 'til I get back. Don't get up from this rock, okay? Will you promise Daddy that?"

She nodded, then sprang to her feet and flung her arms around his neck. "I love you, Daddy," she said, her voice cracking with emotion.

'I love you too, Angel." Pulling back from her, he pushed her to a sitting position and kissed her forehead a second time. Then, he rose and sprinted away just as another call for help echoed across the water.

When he reached the edge of the playground, he dropped to his knees, shaking with exhaustion. He heard footsteps and looked up to see the woman charging toward him.

"My son's foot's stuck," she said gasping for breath. "It's swelling really bad. I tried to pull it loose, but I think I made it worse."

Matt jumped to his feet and raced across the sand to the play station. He scampered up the support ladder and crawled through the circular opening to the boy's side. "Take it easy, Son. You're gonna be okay." He looked at the other boy, crouched inches away. "Go take care of your mom."

The boy's left foot was wedged from just below the ankle bone downward between two of the landing's horizontal support bars. Matt wiggled his right hand through the bars and cautiously wrapped it around the front part of the swollen foot. Then, he wiggled his other hand downward behind the heel. He gently worked the entire foot back and forth in a slight rocking motion to gauge how tightly it was stuck.

Not bad, he thought.

He worked his hands free. Then, it hit him! Earlier, he had seen what looked like a tube of sunscreen on the bench where the woman had been sitting. He glanced around. Sure enough, a copper tone tube lay providentially on the arm of the bench.

"Bring me your sunscreen," Matt said, pointing.

The woman ran and grabbed the tube then hurried back to Matt. He opened the cap, squeezed a profuse amount of the sleek lotion into the palm of one hand, and rubbed his hands together vigorously. Easing them through the bars and around the boy's foot, he lathered as much of its top and sides as he could. Then, he squeezed out more and pasted it on the metal bars.

"Here we go, Buddy," Matt said.

"I'm ready," the boy replied, grimacing.

Methodically, Matt moved the puffy and angry-looking foot back and forth. He felt it loosen a little more with each to and fro motion. After two minutes of painstaking labor, he was able to work the foot free.

The two scooted through the crawl tube to its outer opening. Matt cradled the boy in his arms and carried him to the bench.

"Thank you *so* much," the woman said, kneeling to inspect her son's injury. "Who's your little girl with?"

"She's by herself," Matt said timidly. "I was afraid to bring her with me."

The woman stared at Matt like he had just told her the President had been shot. Then, she jumped to her feet and hurriedly shook his hand. "Go! Hurry!" she commanded. "Me and Zack can get him to the truck. Get back to your daughter!"

A speck of red. That's what he longed to see. Angel's red pullover top standing out against a backdrop of green, brown, and grey foliage, triumphantly proclaiming her safety. His adrenaline surged as he charged up the incline and over the knoll. Seconds later, he would see red and all would be well.

His stride lessened. But the thumping of his heart intensified to the point he thought his chest would explode. He blinked his eyes rapidly, over and over, thinking he was overlooking what his eyes so desperately sought to see. But as he drew near to the rock where he had left her, a numbing reality sank in. There was no red. And no Angel.

Wait! She's playing hide and seek. A sense of relief washed over him. *That has to be it,* he convinced himself.

"Angel?" he yelled.

No response. He called again.

"Angel, we don't have time to play. Come on out."

His eyes scanned the woods for movement. Suddenly, a sound caught his ear. Turning, he noticed water rippling just beyond the pier. Then, the sound repeated, louder and more distinct. It was the quack of a duck.

"Daisy," he whispered.

He walked toward the pier yelling Angel's name over and over. Still no answer. It was not until he reached the pier that he saw them. Five, fluffy yellow ducklings paddling in circles near their mother. Then, he saw something else just inches from the momma duck. Bobbing up and down on the water, its color and shape were mysteriously out of place. Even odder were the faint and intermittent twinkles that radiated from it. Then, he recognized it. A baby blue flip flop with yellow-gold sequins!

OH GOD, NO!

In a fit of unbridled panic, he barreled up the pier's steps and halfway down its span. He wrenched free of his running shoes just before he launched headfirst into the lake, but not before he noticed something else floating inches away from the blue sandal. A bright red hair bow.

The water was cloudy and suffocating. An abyss of gloom and torture. He twisted and groped, moving this way then that, legs kicking, arms flailing, hands searching frantically for any trace of his child. Nothing. He swam deeper. The water was cooler and darker with an oily feel. His limbs began to ache. His lungs screamed for air.

I have to breathe!

With a burst of reserved strength, he propelled upward and broke through to the surface. Treading, he gulped air. Catching his breath, he cried out.

"Oh, God! Please! Don't take my baby!"

He flipped over and descended again. The water seemed more combative than before, like an enemy fended off once, now sensing victory in round two. The thought of his Angel in this murky dungeon nauseated him. But he kept on—plunging, searching, and surfacing, over and over, in a harrowing and vicious cycle. Finally, his body spent, and his heart crushed, he slogged out of the water and collapsed face down on the shore.

It was then the anger consumed him. His wet frame shook with fury as he pounded his fists against the hard ground. He rolled over, writhing in agony, and cried out indignantly to his Heavenly Father.

"Why God?" he wailed. "Is this punishment?"

Seconds turned to minutes and his sobbing steadily faded. He sat up and stared at the space of water that had swallowed up his child. Seized by renewed rage, he grabbed a fistful of the pebbly gravel resting at his feet and flung it across the water. Daisy quacked loudly and herded her ducklings away from the slumped and threatening figure on shore. Then, oblivious to the calamity their presence had just wrought, mother and babies paddled leisurely around the pier and out of sight.

ONE YEAR LATER

CHAPTER ONE

Saturday, June 8, 2013, 7:30 P.M.

Matt raked his half-eaten supper into the disposal and dropped the plate in the sink. He stared out the window at a familiar sight that, in springs past, had been pleasing to look at. Bearded irises framed by coral drift roses and orange day lilies, all of which had exploded with color over the past few weeks. But now, the once-scenic spot sat cursed by two strands of rope and a wooden board that had become a thorn in his flesh.

Day after day she had stood there, pushing the mindless contraption back and forth, back and forth, all the while humming the tune to "Hush Little Baby". Now, after a full year of witnessing the pathetic routine, it had reached a breaking point with him.

It's gotta go, he told himself.

He turned and walked to the end of the bar. Just feet away, Carol sat hushed and sullen, toying with what remained of her dinner. In the room a tension hung in the air, one heavy enough that, in his mind, the steak knife to the right of her hand could slice through.

"We have to talk," he said firmly.

Her hand grew still. She looked up and, with empty eyes, stared into her husband's. "About?"

"I think you know what about," Matt replied.

Carol's gaze shifted back to her plate. "I'm listening," she said flatly.

Matt walked back to the window. He gripped the edge of the counter. "We can't go on like this. The church deserves better than what we've given them the past year."

Total silence. Again, he turned to face her.

"It's time we moved on."

She leaned back slightly and pushed her plate forward. "Easy for you to say," she said, her tone now laced with sarcasm.

Her callous reply hit hard. Deep inside him, a tiny spark of anger began to flame. "You're not the only one in this house who's been grieving, you know. Losing her's been hard on me, too."

She slammed her fork to her plate and pounded the table with her fist. Her head jerked sideways to face him head on. "Well, in case you've forgot, let me remind you that you're the one who left her by herself that day. To run to help some kid—"

"I'm taking the swing down," he announced, stopping her mid-sentence.

As the words escaped him, he felt the air in the room thicken. Carol pushed back her chair and sprang to her feet. As she charged toward him, the veins in her neck pulsated, her face growing redder with each step. When she was within an arm's reach of him, her hate-filled eyes stared into his. She pointed past him through the window.

"That swing is the only thing I have left of her. How dare you even think about taking it down!"

Matt steeled himself. "Honey, it's keeping you from getting on with your life. It's got—"

"YOU KILLED HER!"

Inside him, the flame of anger suddenly exploded into all-out wrath. With teeth clenched and chin set, he raised his arm and flattened his palm, poised to deliver a blow that would crush her will and restore his dominance. Then, time seemed to freeze. Except for over the past year, when they had been shadowed in despair, he had always seen love in her eyes. Now, he saw something he had never seen before, something that cut him to the quick. He saw fear—fear of ***him***.

He lowered his arm to his side. For a few tense seconds, the two stood facing each other, locked in a duel of silence. Then, a harsh and jarring reality hit him. He had come perilously close to hitting the woman he had vowed to protect on his wedding day.

Carol covered her face and broke into sobs. Before he could speak, she turned and fled to the bedroom, slamming the door behind her. After a long and guilt-ridden minute, he made his way to the couch and collapsed, his mind still dazed by what had just happened. Down the hall, he could hear the love of his life wailing and weeping, a sound that sickened him to his core.

Minutes turned to hours. The sobs faded as darkness slowly overtook the house. Finally, as the hall clock struck midnight, he fell asleep.

Six hours later, the scream of an ambulance siren jolted him awake. He sat up and stroked the four-day stubble that had sprouted across his chin, lower jaws, and down the contours of his neck. He ran his fingers through his peppered black hair and scratched his scalp vigorously. Sleeping on the couch had grown old. For the better part of a year now, the master bedroom and bath had been off limits. The hall bathroom boasted only a small, four-decades old cast iron tub that didn't fit his six-foot, two-inch frame. So, he had retreated to the church for his daily shower and shave. Since Wednesday, though, he had shunned all manner of hygiene, his musty skin now a stark reminder. He was an unwanted guest in his own house. And that had to end...soon!

He slipped on his brown loafers and crept quietly through the kitchen and out the door. He grabbed his heavy-duty loppers from the storage cabinet, then headed to the large pin oak in the back yard. As he stared at the swing, his heart ached. Once vibrant and alive with an energy all its own, it now hung lifeless and decrepit, its ropes frayed and dingy brown. And the wooden seat, at one time shiny from high-gloss redwood stain, had lost all its sheen and appeared close to buckling.

He raised the loppers to one of the ropes and extended the handles outward to open the blades. Suddenly, he stopped. Maybe it was repressed anger. Or a surge of masculinity. Whatever it was that gripped him inside, he seized it with a grit and a passion that momentarily turned him into a man of steel.

He would conquer this enemy with his bare hands.

He flung the loppers to the ground and grabbed the ropes, one in each fist, and pulled—once, twice, three times. Feeling the nylon start to weaken, he yanked harder, again and again. He paused briefly to catch his breath and wipe the sweat from his forehead. Then, he renewed the assault, tugging with all the brute strength he could muster. Over and over, he heaved, letting go of a year's worth of frustration. He felt the rope burning his hands, but he didn't care. With a final burst of adrenaline, he pulled with all his might and the ropes separated from the branch. He tumbled backward and fell hard on his backside with the ropes in his hands and the board at his feet.

He lay still, processing his feat. Strangely, the ground beneath him felt soft and soothing, as if complimenting his heroic effort.

After a few minutes, he rose and carried the swing to his truck. After placing it in the truck bed, he hurriedly drove away.

On his way to the church, questions rumbled through his head. How long before Carol noticed? How would she react? Should he have waited until tomorrow? He assured himself over and over he had done the right thing. After all, today marked one year since the accident.

And it was time to move on.

CHAPTER TWO

Sunday Morning, 7:38 A.M.

Carol turned on the cold water and cupped the stream into a small pool. She raised it to her face. For a moment her troubles washed away. Then, last night's pow wow with Matt replayed inside her head. She felt her blood boil.

How could he even think of such a thing?

She grabbed a drying towel from the rack and dabbed her face. As she placed the towel on the vanity, the image staring back at her from the mirror gave her pause. What reason did that woman have to go on living? Would she ever have a reason again?

She slipped her chenille robe on over her pajamas and trudged to the kitchen. Pressing the brew button on the coffee machine, she grabbed her pink cup from the mug tree next to it. As she waited with closed eyes, the familiar gurgle seemed to offer a strange solace. After a minute of quiet and calm, she filled the mug and stared intently at the dark liquid. Its warmth and aroma wafted upward to her nose.

She set the cup down, opened the utensil drawer to her right, and lifted out a teaspoon. Black was how she usually liked her coffee. But today she needed a change. She stirred a package of sweetener into the mug and watched as the inky liquid consumed the tiny white granules. Would a few ounces of fake sugar sweeten her drab and sour life?

She raised the cup to her lips, glanced out the window—and gasped in horror! *He did it!* Her knees grew weak. Her hands went limp. And the mug dropped to the counter's edge, shattering and sending hot coffee onto her robe, the tile floor, and into the sink. She grabbed the edge of the countertop in an attempt to steady herself, but the shock was too much. Trembling, she collapsed to the floor.

"How could he?" she screamed as the tears rushed forth. The one thing that had given her any comfort, he had yanked away. The one spot on earth where she found any peace, he had defiled. As her tears rained down on the hard, cold floor, an odd truth struck her. The ceramic shards, the tiny puddles, the whole mess in which she sat—it mimicked her own life. A life broken and spilled out.

She wiped her eyes on the sleeve of her robe and leaned back against the cabinet. Then, she looked heavenward and cried out to the One she had shut out of her life for so long.

"God help me! Please!"

Matt emerged from the bathroom off his study dressed in grey dockers, a white pinstriped button-down shirt, and black loafers. Fresh from a hot shower and a shave, he felt relaxed and revitalized. He stared down at the palms of his hands. Still raw from pulling on the rope, they were coated in Porter's salve he had found in the bottom drawer of the bathroom vanity only two weeks ago. At the time, he had come close to tossing the tiny tin container in the trash. Now he wondered if providence had intervened in a most subtle way. The thought evoked both a grin and a mute laugh.

He settled into his swivel chair and looked around the room. When he had arrived as the new pastor of Grace Fellowship Church twenty years ago, dark paneling and dull green shag carpet had greeted him in this office. He had waited fifteen years, until the carpet had worn exceedingly thin, before asking for something more contemporary. Now his feet rested on plush, chocolate-colored fabric that his shoes sank into. And the once-dark paneled walls were now decorated with a faux design that lent a gentle ambiance to the room. The setting was modest but hallowed. And through the years it had been filled with words and actions ranging from the humorous to the dramatic to the life changing.

He leaned forward, planted his elbows on the desk, then joined his hands to rest his chin on his locked fingers.

She knows by now.

A cold dread washed over him. In his head, he could hear the piercing scream and the blubbering that had no doubt followed. Had she thrown anything? Would there be a wall to repair?

He stared at his cell phone lying just inches away from his reluctant hands. Would she answer? He bit his lip and strummed his fingers on the desk.

Just do it.

He pulled his handkerchief from his back pocket and dabbed the salve from his hands, then dialed her number and waited. With each ring, he felt his heart quicken.

"What?" she answered coldly.

Matt grimaced and leaned back in his chair. He rubbed his fingers across his forehead hoping to somehow push the right words into his brain.

"Carol, I know you're upset. But what I did. It's best for you and for us," he said in the sincerest tone he could muster.

He held his breath and braced himself for a biting comeback. An eerie silence followed. Against his ear the phone suddenly felt hot like it had been charged with her anger. He exhaled and continued.

"I'm sorry about last night. No man should behave like that. I hope you'll forgive me."

Again, a long silence. "Are you still there?"

"I'm here," she replied softly. "Matt, I'm not feeling well. If I don't make it for the service, apologize to the congregation for me."

"I understand if you're not up to it," he said mildly. "Try to at least come for the potluck meal. The ladies have worked really hard on the fellowship hall. You'll love the way it's decorated, especially the pink carnations."

Pink was her favorite color. And live flowers always found a soft spot with her. Would the allure of both melt her heart?

"We'll see," she said aloofly. Then, a silence that told him she was gone.

CHAPTER THREE

Sunday Morning, 8:40 A.M.

The thought of Carol not showing up on this special day was sobering. And, in his heart, Matt couldn't help but feel angry that she would choose to ignore the efforts of the congregation that had supported them for two decades. *What will I tell them?* he asked himself. A made-up excuse? No, he would tell his church the truth. That even after a year, grief still controlled her.

He reached down and pulled out the bottom drawer of his desk. His fingers crept under a stack of manila folders, searching for something that had lain hidden for almost a year. As his flesh contacted its smooth grain, a tingle shot down his spine.

His eyes clenched shut as he pulled it from the drawer. Placing it on the desk in front of him, he rested his fingertips on it and stroked its texture while keeping his eyes closed.

He opened them. Staring back at him was the face of an angel—his Angel. Her black shoulder-length curls wet from splashing in water. Her blue eyes glowing with excitement. And that impish grin—the one that had melted his daddy heart time and time again. Even now, he could hear the glee in her voice.

"Promise me we can come back and swim again, Daddy?"

"I promise," Matt had told her.

Already on edge about her baby's safety, Carol had shot him a look of defiance. And in that moment he told himself he had just made a promise he might end up having to break.

If only I had broke it, he mused.

He raised the picture to his lips and kissed it. "I love you, Angel" he whispered softly.

"Nickel for your thoughts?" a familiar voice said.

Startled, Matt looked up. "Hey, Chuck," he replied. "I was a million miles away."

A sixty-eight-year-old army veteran with a scarred walk to prove it, Chuck Wilkins was one of Matt's most faithful church members. He lived in a crumbling, depression-era house just outside of town and was usually the first to arrive—rain or shine—on foot every Sunday morning. A solitary man with no living bloodline, Chuck had forged a remarkable bond with his pastor over the past two decades. As he was quick to tell the church folks, "Me and the preacher's as close as brothers."

"Have a seat," Matt said, motioning to the chair in front of him. He quickly grabbed Angel's picture by its corner and dropped it in his lap. Then, as Chuck ambled forward, Matt discreetly placed the picture back in the open drawer and closed it.

"How was the walk into town this morning? From what I saw, the sunrise sure did look like a pretty one."

"One of the grandest I've seen in a long time," Chuck replied through a toothy grin. "There's somethin' special about the sun comin' up. It's like God's first smile of the day."

Matt took close note of his friend. The years were fast taking their toll on this man that had defended his country so proudly. His time in Vietnam had cost Chuck dearly. But you'd never hear him complain or begrudge the lead shrapnel that had spewed from a land mine during a skirmish outside Saigon and now lay embedded in his right leg. A hidden badge of honor, Chuck called it. And he was always quick to tell anyone interested or not that he would do it all over again to defend the land he loved.

"I sure wish you'd rub off on some of our church members," Matt said. "Some of them see the sun risin' and dread what the day holds."

Noticeably winded, Chuck laughed as he sat down and pushed back the wispy gray bangs that hung loosely down his forehead. He positioned his challenged limb at just the right angle to avoid discomfort.

"Lighten' up, Preacher. Some folks think life ought to be rosy all the time. Now how dull would that be?"

"Sometimes I think you missed your callin', Buddy. You should have been a preacher yourself."

Matt envied his friend. Chuck was such a simple man. But he possessed a wit and an insight Matt could only dream of.

Chuck's expression suddenly grew solemn. "So, it's been a year today. You gotta' be hurtin', my friend. Wanna talk about it?"

"Thanks for askin'," Matt began. "I'd be lyin' if I told you it was any better." He pointed to the left side of his chest. "There's an ache in here I'm not sure'll ever go away. I've heard all my life that time heals. But so far, I'm not feelin' any mendin' goin' on. It's like the wound's still open."

Chuck shifted in his seat and crossed his arms. "What about Carol? She still blamin' you?"

"She's still holds me responsible. I don't know if she'll ever forgive me." His voice grew somber as a tear spilled down his cheek. "I'm worried about her, Chuck. Sometimes I think she's lost her will to live. Every day is a battle for her—and for us. I can't talk to her about it. She shuts off when I try to. And she throws any kindness I try to show her back at me. I don't know what to do."

Chuck leaned forward and extended his right arm. "Take my hand, Brother."

Matt gripped the outstretched hand. Chuck's words gripped his pastor's heart.

"You're gonna make it through this, Preacher. And when it's over you'll be stronger for it. I know about goin' through a battle. There were some nights the gunfire was so close I thought I wouldn't see mornin'. But I kept tellin' myself the fight wouldn't kill me, that I'd make it back home. And here I am."

He pulled a handkerchief from the rear pocket of his jeans and wiped a tear from his face. "Don't give up, Brother. You've got a congregation supportin' you. You've got a wife that loves you. She may not be showin' it right now, but she does love you. And you've got a faith that's strong. Remember, you've gotta go through battles to win a war."

Matt released Chuck's grip and made his way around the desk. "Thank you, Chuck. I don't know what I'd do without your friendship."

Chuck drew his pastor close. "Just remember," he said. "Jesus cried, too.

CHAPTER FOUR

Sunday Morning, 9:05 A.M.

Carol's cell phone vibrated inside the pocket of her robe. She stared down at its screen and saw a text message that for the first time in a long time brought a smile to her face.

> Hey GF! Big day ahead. Left yet?

Linda, her best friend in the whole world. Her solid rock that had stood by her for the past year. During that awful span, many she had counted as friends hadn't found the time for her. Some had glaringly avoided her. A few had all but told her in cold and callous words to get over it and move on. Still others, though well-intentioned, had offered kind words she knew were relevant, but it hadn't been what she wanted to hear. All of them, either through their withdrawal or their futile attempts at condolence, had touched her. Many in ways she would never forget. Some in ways she would likely never get over.

One had remained constant and steadfast. Linda Stevens—the one woman she could always count on. Her soulmate, confidante, and sister. Had it not been for Linda, Carol was convinced she would be locked away somewhere right now, restrained in a straitjacket in a dark room with padded walls. Her body wasting away. Her mind adrift in a sea of misery and confusion. But Linda had cared enough to see that didn't happen. For twelve long months she had been there for her best friend, sacrificing in her own life to make sure Carol didn't wander down a path of self-destruction. Linda Stevens had saved her life.

I can't let her down, she said in a half-whisper. But the thought of playing the role of devoted pastor's wife when she was in such a rotten mood made her wince with disgust.

What do I do? She screamed the words at the woman staring back from the bathroom mirror in front of her but got no answer.

She studied her reflection. What a pathetic sight she was! Her eyes were bloodshot and puffy from the bout of crying earlier. Her shoulder-length, honey blonde hair, unwashed since Tuesday, hung in matted strings about her shoulders. And her usually creamy complexion looked as pale as that of a corpse ready for the grave. It was time for a fast makeover.

She tapped her finger on the message bar of her phone.

> Not yet. C U in a bit

She would go. For Linda, not for him.

Matt stepped into the sanctuary. *Lord, let this be a time of renewal,* he prayed silently. *And let her show up.*

He looked around the room and drank in the warmth of the scene in front of him. Pleasing conversation filled the air like the muffled hum of a bee swarm. Random laughter could be heard above the steady drone. Shades of the past two decades overwhelmed him. He felt painfully unworthy of the moment, so unfit to lead this precious body.

"Well, either they still love you or they came to eat," Chuck said, interrupting his pastors' reverie.

"Don't be so hard on me, Brother" Matt replied, smiling lopsidedly. He knew Chuck was joking, but deep down he wondered how many in the building his comment fit.

In front of the pulpit stood his seven-member deacon board. Seldom seen in anything but jeans and casual shirts, all were decked out in oldfangled suits and gawdy neckties. "This is gonna be fun," he said, winking at Chuck.

"Well, look at you guys," Matt said jovially. "I must say you fellas do clean up rather well. Did you guys dress yourselves or did your wives do it?"

Jerry Mitchell, chairman of the deacon board, was the first to counter. "Actually, Delores is pretty good at fancyin' up a man—and tyin' a tie. I did have to bribe her, though. Told her I'd take her to Texarkana tomorrow night to eat. After bein' married for thirty-two years, I've learned one thing. Treatin' your wife to a night on the town gets you points." Jerry raised his dark, bushy eyebrows, anticipating assent from the rest of the group. The other men quickly nodded.

Gabe Adams, the youngest deacon and a confirmed local yokel, chimed in. "I hadn't had this suit on since I got married." He opened the visibly snug coat to reveal a white shirt that looked like it could pop open at any second. "Tried to tie this tie a half a dozen times. Finally, Susie wrapped it around me and had it tied in thirty seconds. 'Bout choked me when she tightened it up. Don't tell her, but I loosened it some." He grimaced and pulled it farther away from his neck. "She told me I owed her. I'll figure somethin' out."

"You guys hang around after the potluck for a picture. I doubt you'll ever look this good again," Matt chuckled.

Then, out of the blue, came the question he had been dreading. "Where's Carol?"

Jerry's words stabbed the air with a punch, jolting Matt back to the reality of the moment. A burning sensation spread slowly upward from his neck all the way to his forehead.

"She's been under the weather since Thursday. Headache mostly. I talked with her a little while ago. She should be here any minute." Part of it was true, enough that Matt felt temporarily absolved. She had been fighting a headache. And he had talked to her earlier.

Dear God, let her show up!

Jerry glanced at his watch. "It's about time to kick this thing off." He pointed to the two wingback chairs that usually sat on either side of the platform but had been moved forward and placed side by side. "You and your Missus will be front and center for the next hour."

Matt took his seat in the chair nearest the lectern. Jerry sat in the other one and leaned in. "I'm gonna open up with a prayer, welcome everybody, then talk about your twenty years here. Then a few others have some things they want to share. There's some special music along the way, too. And a short slide show." He patted Matt's shoulder. "Then we'll eat."

His eyes panned the auditorium. "I still don't see Carol. Do you think we need to call her?"

"She's not coming, Jerry."

The words escaped Matt before he could temper them with any remorse. He stared downward, ashamed to look his friend in the eye. Out of the corner of his eye, he saw Jerry signal to Ellen Monroe to play through another chorus of "Victory in Jesus".

"Why not?" Jerry finally managed to ask. "Is she sick?"

"No," Matt said faintly, shaking his head. "She's mad at me."

He grabbed Jerry's arm. "I'm so sorry. I don't know what else to say."

"What do I tell 'em?" Jerry asked, gesturing toward the congregation. "They've been preparin' this for months." He gazed upward as if waiting for a divine revelation. "Any ideas?"

Matt knew what he had to do. It wasn't Jerry's place to tell the church. It was his. And for the first time in months, he felt relieved that, as their shepherd, he would finally be able to share the truth.

"I've got this," Matt said, rising to his feet. Giving Jerry no chance to reply, he stepped to the lectern. As the buzz from the crowd slowly died down, Matt remembered the words of Matthew 10:20: "For it will not be you speaking, but the Spirit of your Father speaking through you."

No, he didn't have this. God did.

CHAPTER FIVE

Sunday Morning, 9:35 A.M.

He had stood in this spot hundreds of times. But as he grasped the corners of the lectern, the edgy silence that fell over the crowd made Matt feel like a stranger in the normally friendly confines of the auditorium.

"Before we get started this morning, there's some things I need to tell of all of you." He paused to clear his throat. "One year ago today, my life changed forever. Before then, I'd been told that burying a child is the hardest thing a person can do. I can't agree more. A part of me is gone that I'll never get back."

"But I'm not the only one who's struggled over the past year. Carol's struggled, too. Even worse than I have. She prayed so long for a child. Angela was the answer to that prayer. Then, losing her the way we did..."

Matt's voice trailed off as those words echoed through his head. *"LOSING HER THE WAY WE DID."* A fresh reminder of the truth. And suddenly that painful truth came surging back with a vengeance, weakening his frame and confounding his mind. He renewed his grip on the lectern and raised his upper body slightly to stabilize his trembling legs. But he couldn't shake the images of that terrible day. Angela had died because of **HIS** negligence. **HE** was responsible for the veil of grief that now overshadowed his ministry and threatened his marriage. His daughter's blood would forever be on **HIS** hands.

Picking up where he had left off, Matt continued, his voice slightly raised and a bit more assertive.

"Carol's hurting. Really hurting. For the past year I've not been the husband I should have been. In fact, I've failed miserably. Our life as a couple's been very strained. I'm doing my best to regain her trust and her love. And as your pastor, I've not been the leader I should have been. I hope you can forgive me."

A strange sensation slowly began to creep over him, beginning at head level and making its way downward through his torso. All at once, his vision grew fuzzy as the air around him took on a grayness that seemed to shroud him in a vacuum. From somewhere deep within, he pulled forth the strength to continue.

"Carol won't be here today."

There. He had finally said what he had been putting off saying. But the words seemed to have echoed off the back wall of the auditorium, causing him to wonder if he had actually said them. He paused, perplexed by the lack of reaction to his admission. Had they heard him? They appeared motionless and stoic, unmoved by his revelation.

What's happening, he asked himself.

Suddenly, the air around him grew even hazier, charged with an electricity that seemed to engulf him. After mouthing the words "I'm sorry", he released his grip on the lectern and turned and stared at the chair he had left only minutes earlier. It was feet away, but it seemed oddly out of reach. He took one step toward it then froze. Through cloudy eyes, he saw Jerry spring to his feet and extend both arms outward. Then......

Blackness.

Carol grabbed her suede clutch off the bar and hurriedly made her way across the kitchen and through the laundry room. As her hand reached for the handle of the storm door that led out to the carport, a familiar sound stopped her in her tracks. The chorus to <u>We are Family</u>—Linda's ringtone. *That's strange,* she thought. A quick glance at her watch showed 9:51. As the Sledge Sisters belted out the timeless tune, Carol's mind raced. The service had to be underway by now. And she and Linda had texted only minutes earlier. She opened the clutch and dug for the ringing phone.

"Linda?"

The voice at the other end was raised and pressing, not the soft, calm one she was used to.

"Where are you?" Linda was all but shrieking as she spit the words out. "Why aren't you here?"

Before Carol could answer, she heard her best friend break into sobs. *Surely, she's not crying because I'm late,* she wondered. Linda could be emotional at times. But she was a nurse, calloused by years of watching people hurt and suffer. No, something else had to be going on.

"I'm walking out the door right now. Linda, what's wrong?"

As she waited for a response, Carol grabbed the edge of the cabinet top near her with her free hand to brace herself.

"Matt passed out a few minutes ago. He's still unconscious."

As Linda's words rattled through her head, Carol stood riveted. Had she heard right?

"Passed out? Why?" She winced as she realized how foolish her 'Why' must have sounded.

"I don't know WHY," Linda replied, annoyance evident in her voice. "Just get here fast. We need you!"

"I'm on my way."

As she opened the door to her SUV and settled in behind the steering wheel, the scene waiting for her played inside her head. Somewhere in the sanctuary, her husband lay unconscious. Around him were gathered a few pious men who considered themselves his inner circle. The remainder of the flock was likely clustered in cliquish bunches, some lamenting the plight of their pastor, others assessing the faults of his wife. And her best friend the nurse was kneeling beside Matt, doing what she could to rouse him.

As she drove the few short blocks to the church, there was no hastening, no urgency, and no worry. Her foot, normally heavy on the accelerator, rested lightly against it, buying time. And when the pastor's wife finally pulled into the parking lot south of the church sanctuary, only one thought prevailed.

Duty calls.

Matt woke to find Linda Stevens dabbing his forehead with a damp cloth. As he gazed upward, his eyes focused in on the faded brown beams some twenty-five feet up. Just feet away, he heard men talking and recognized Jerry's gravelly voice along with the smoother pitches of Chuck's and Linda's son Brett. Gradually, the reality of what had just happened sank in. Matt groaned deeply, more out of regret than discomfort.

Could this day get any worse?

"You gave us quite a scare," Linda said. "How do you feel?"

"A little dazed," Matt replied, attempting to rise. With her help, he righted himself, bending his legs and planting his hands on the soft red carpet. "Can't figure out what brought that on. I've never fainted in my life."

"You've been under a lot of stress, Pastor," Jerry said. "And with this bein' the anniversary...with it bein' BOTH anniversaries and all, it was just too much on you. You feel okay? You think you need to go to the ER?"

"I'll be fine," Matt said as he leaned back and rested his head against the wooden partition separating the pulpit area from the choir loft. He stared straight ahead and saw that the pews were empty. Had everyone gone home?

"They're all in the fellowship hall," Chuck said. "We didn't see any reason for 'em to stay in here. It's gettin' close to eatin' time, anyway."

Sudden movement caught Matt's eye. He looked toward the piano and watched as Carol entered through the double glass doors on the south wall. Her pace was stroll-like as she made her way forward and walked up the three narrow steps to the raised platform.

"How's he doing?"she asked, her tone tepid.

"He's back with us, Aunt Carol," Brett said. "Looks like he's gonna be okay."

"Help me up," Matt said, extending his hand toward Brett. The strapping teen grabbed his pastor by the hand and pulled him up with ease. Matt clutched the back of his head and felt a lump behind his left ear where his head had hit the floor. He flinched in pain as his fingers massaged the tender spot. With Brett's help, he edged toward the chair where Jerry had sat minutes earlier.

"Thank you, Son," he said, smiling at the young man he and Carol had been godparents to for over seventeen years. His face grew solemn, and he stared at the floor. "I'd like to be alone with Carol. Y'all go on back."

"Sure, Pastor," Jerry replied. "Take your time."

When they were alone, Matt looked at Carol. Picking up where they had left off the night before, the two stared icily at each other. Despite her cold demeanor, Matt couldn't help but notice how beautiful his wife looked. Not a hair out of place. Make-up impeccably applied. Manicured nails. And the black satin dress she wore, accented by a multi-colored, silk scarf, complemented her looks to perfection. *What a contrast,* Matt thought, *between the outside and the inside.*

"Thanks for coming," Matt said. "It means a lot."

Carol raised her hands and planted them firmly on her hips, her elbows turned outward. Her response was dour and forbidding.

"Let's get something straight. I'm not here because I want to be. I'm here because I'm expected to be—as the dutiful preacher's wife. And as hard as Linda's worked on all this, I couldn't let *her* down."

A brazen grin spread across her face as she allowed her scathing words to soak in. In a brash tone, she continued.

"So, let's just get through this, okay. Let's put on our best faces and go back there and do what we have to do."

"Okay," he agreed. "But would it be asking too much for us to walk in holding hands?"

A mix of shock and surprise colored her face. "I don't think so."

With Carol deliberately trailing him by two paces, the two slowly made their way through the hallways to the waiting crowd. *Another battle lost,* he told himself. But as they neared the entrance to the fellowship hall, Matt heard the swish of her dress draw closer. Then, he felt the soft flesh of her hand against his.

How he had missed that touch! It had eluded him for so long it now felt a bit foreign. A smile creased his lips as she locked her fingers with his. He longed to turn, to see if she was smiling, too.

Instead, he stared straight ahead, savoring the intimacy that would fade just around the corner when their hands parted.

Was this a watershed moment? Could a simple joining of hands spell the end of a year marred by grief and the start of a future filled with promise? Matt wasn't sure. All he knew was at this moment, his wife was by his side. And a few steps farther, he would join a couple hundred people who had become his extended family. Together, they would partake of the tasty treats whose aroma even now was tempting his taste buds. And somewhere among all those delicacies, waiting just for the preacher, was a slice of Ms. Wilma Thomas' prize-winning lemon pie with its towering meringue. All things considered, for a middle-aged man of the cloth who was quick to count his blessings, life didn't get much better than this!

Matt pulled his truck off Perkins Street and drove slowly down the asphalt trail that looped through Memorial Gardens. On the back side of the cemetery, he veered into a small clearing covered with loose gravel. Killing the engine, he sat quietly for several minutes recounting the events of the last two hours. The long-awaited celebration was over. Now his congregation knew what a mess his life was in. But, as he had expected, they had pledged their love and support in helping him and Carol move forward. And something told him he hadn't confessed anything they didn't already know.

As he made his way through the gravestones jutting up from the ground, he ordered his steps carefully, making sure not to tread where coffins and their sacred contents rested six feet down. As he neared his destination, his pace slackened. Tension suddenly welled within him, and he considered turning back. But an invisible force pushed him forward until he stood at the foot of his daughter's grave.

The granite had weathered considerably over the past twelve months. The mound of dirt that had silently announced the gravesite for the first few months was now reduced to a slight hump, grass covering all but a small oval-shaped spot just above the footstone. And the ornate concrete bench, a memorial from the church body, sat askew as if someone's full weight had rested on one end.

He walked to the headstone and knelt, reaching out to caress the glass that covered the image of his Angel. Then, drained by the events of the past hours, he lowered his body to a sitting position and leaned against the smooth vertical surface of the monument.

For a long time, he sat motionless, his musing interrupted only by the sporadic cooing of a mourning dove nearby. After a half hour, he stood to his feet and walked briskly back to his truck. As he circled the northeast corner of the gardens and arrived back at Perkins Street, a sense of resolve settled over him. He couldn't change the past. But with God's help, he could carve out a future. A future of hope and promise for him and the woman he loved. He needed Carol. And she needed him. They were a team called to lead a body of New Testament believers. And there was no higher calling for a farm-boy-turned-pastor, he reminded himself.

Lord willing, things were about to change. Starting now.

CHAPTER SIX

Sunday Afternoon, 2:58 P.M

The scent of household cleaner tinged with the faint aroma of coffee hung in the kitchen air. As Matt's eyes panned the dimly lit room, he spied something out of place under the cabinet doors to the right of the sink. He made his way across the hard tile and crouched low. As his fingers made contact with the object's surface, a twinge of pain coursed through him. He winced and drew his hand upward. Blood oozed from a linear cut along the side of his thumb.

He dropped to his knees and scrabbled out what had just bit him. It was dull pink in color and easily recognizable. The handle to Carol's coffee mug. Severed and sharp where it had once attached to the side of the cup. The one he had bought her not long after they had moved to town. It hadn't been her birthday or their anniversary or any other special event. It had been one of those "just because" occasions. Embossed with a black "C", it had caught his eye while he had browsed through an outdoor flea market at Southtown Plaza years earlier. How she had fretted over it from the start!

He could still hear her heartfelt declaration when he had given it to her. "I'll always drink my coffee out of this cup. And I'll think of you every time I use it."

Now, as he held the ear-shaped fragment in his hand, he wondered if her once-prized token had been reduced to pieces during a tantrum only hours earlier. Or had something less blistering turned it into collateral damage?

Rising, Matt placed the ceramic piece on the countertop and turned on the sink's cold tap. He ran his hand under the cool water to wash away the blood that by now had trickled to the base of his thumb. He pulled a paper towel from its holder and pressed it against the cut. After a few seconds, the red flow dried up.

The hall clock clanged a trio of chimes, announcing the three o'clock hour. He grabbed the mug handle by its smooth curve and using his fingernails, meticulously chipped away at its ragged points until the sharp edges were gone, then positioned it ring-like around his index finger.

It's time, he told himself.

As he made his way down the carpeted hallway to the master bedroom, his muffled steps slowed, and his heart raced slightly. Minutes earlier he had felt a rush of confidence about this. Now a sense of unease swept over him.

She sat on the side of the bed still dressed in church clothes, cradling a framed portrait in her hands. Seeing the bare spot on the nightstand, he knew immediately which picture it was: Angel just one week shy of her first birthday wearing a red dress with a matching scarlet bow perched atop her black curls. *Maybe this is not the time*, he thought.

He watched as she caressed the smooth glass, her gaze fixated on the image of her deceased child.

No, he told himself. *It can't wait any longer.*

He took a deep breath. "Hey."

Carol winced and looked up, her face awash with surprise. She clutched the picture to her chest and stared at the floor. "I didn't hear you come in," she said, placing the picture back on the nightstand.

Her upper body relaxed a bit, and she clasped her hands together and lowered them to her lap.

Matt's legs felt wobbly, and he leaned against the doorframe. His fingers toyed with the cup handle, and he asked himself why he had brought it with him. Was it some sort of strange peace offering?

"I thought you might be sleeping, so I made sure to be extra quiet when I came in," he replied after some quick thinking. "Are you okay?"

A quick read of her body language revealed little. Her stare fixed momentarily on the floor again. Then, she straightened a little and turned her eyes back to Angela's picture.

"Do you remember the day we had that taken? We were so scared she'd be fussy. But you kept making those funny faces at her and she did so good."

A quiet laugh escaped Carol, and she turned back toward him. He had wondered lately if he would ever hear that half giggle, half chuckle again. Now, to hear it and see the closed-lip smile that creased her mouth gave Matt hope. Guarded hope.

"I remember," Matt replied, grinning. "I made the biggest fool of myself that day, but you've gotta admit, it worked."

Carol laughed again, louder and more spirited this time. "It sure did. You had me laughing so hard it hurt. And the photographer was crackin' up, too."

Where was this going?

As he pondered what to say next, she placed her hand on the bed and patted it invitingly. "Come sit by me."

Something was happening. Was she setting him up for a fall? Was she drawing him in so she could lower the boom one more time? And that smile—something about it didn't seem right. Did it mask a still-frosty heart bent on further combat? After all the bickering, after all the coldness, after all the months of silently rubbing shoulders under this same roof, could getting back really be this easy?

Matt walked across the room and sat down an arm's reach from his wife. The bed felt softer than he remembered. He ran his hand gently across the smooth fabric of the comforter. Just to touch it after almost a year made him feel giddy inside. Her voice interrupted his musing.

"What's that on your hand?"

He removed the mug handle from his finger and placed it in his palm. She studied it intently, her puzzled expression soon turning to one of recognition.

"I dropped my mug this morning when I was drinking my coffee," she said meekly. "It was an accident."

An accident? She hadn't deliberately smashed it to the floor in a fit of rage over the swing? Matt wondered. He wasn't so sure.

"Was it *really* an accident?" he asked nervously, turning to face her.

"Of course, it was!" she said, her voice raised and assuring. "You know how much that cup meant to me. I'd never do anything to it on purpose."

She looked away, and the two of them sat quiet for an angst-filled minute. As much as he wanted to know more about what had happened, something told him not to push it.

"I'm sorry I doubted you," he said.

She was lightning fast with her comeback. "What did you do with it?"

The question rattled him for a second. Then, it dawned on him she was asking about the swing. Was this calm exchange about to go downhill fast?

A sudden boldness surged through him, and he edged closer to her. He reached across to take her hand in his. To his surprise, she didn't flinch or resist. Her hand felt warm and cushy, more than it had at the church earlier.

"I put it in the dumpster behind city hall."

She squeezed his hand lightly and stroked the upper part of his thumb with hers. The soft motion sent chills through him. Maybe this wasn't going south after all.

"Would you go get it?"

WHAT?

Disbelief swirled inside his head. Surely, she hadn't asked what he thought he had just heard her ask. As his mind processed the possibility, he was jolted back to reality when she repeated the question.

"Will you go get it?"

With an almost supernatural control, he was able to seize the shock and irritation fast welling within him. This time of mending had come too far to let it slip away now.

"Honey, listen to me. That swing was a stumbling block for both of us. It was a constant reminder, day in and day out, that she's gone. We've got to move on."

"I know," she replied, her body trembling with emotion. "But I want to keep it. I promise I'll leave it alone. Just go get it, Matt. Please?"

Matt laid the ceramic piece on the bed beside him and closed the space between them. He circled her back with his arm and drew her close. He could feel her shaking now and noticed tears flowing freely down her cheeks.

"All right," he conceded. "I'll go get it. But I'm not hangin' it back up. I'm putting it somewhere outta sight."

She nodded in agreement. Matt pulled a handkerchief from the rear pocket of his slacks and handed it to her. She dabbed the tears from her face and folded the cloth double. He massaged her back and she leaned her head against his shoulder.

"Oh Matt! How can we go on without our Angel? How, Matt?"

"One day at a time. That's all we can do. Lean on each other and our church family. We need them now more than ever. And they need us."

The words seemed to resonate with her, and she circled his lower back with her free arm. The two held each other tight for a long time. When they finally broke the embrace, Matt raised the hand he held and gently kissed the back of it. Then, he leaned over and kissed her moistened cheek.

"I love you, Sweetness," he whispered. "Nothing will ever change that."

He looked into her eyes. They were no longer empty and cold. Instead, they radiated a warmth and love that seemed to immerse his soul.

He quickly assessed his position. The way he saw it, the wall that had separated them for the past year had been breached. But, he knew all too well that same wall had not yet crumbled. That would take more giving on his part. And time.

"Why don't you get some rest?" he suggested. "You look exhausted."

She kicked off her shoes and removed the scarf from around her neck. "I could use a nap. It's been a long day."

He retrieved a light-weight razorback throw from the hall closet and draped it lovingly over her as if tucking a child into bed. "I'll check on you later," he whispered, kissing her temple.

He turned to leave. Her words stopped him in his tracks and brought a lump to his throat.

"No couch tonight, Matt."

Closing the door behind him, he stood still, taking in all that had just happened. It felt good, almost too good. Had he missed something?

The hall clock feet away chimed a quarter past three. Fifteen minutes—that's how long it had been since he had first entered the bedroom. In that short window of time, his topsy-turvy world had seemingly undergone a one-eighty. Deep inside, though, he couldn't help but wonder.

Had it really?

Time would tell. Right now, he had a swing to rescue.

End of Part One

CHAPTER SEVEN

Monday June 10th, 7:45 A.M.

Asheville Arkansas is a town going nowhere—size wise anyway. An iron-willed clan of private landowners have seen to that for generations. Through the years they've been courted time and again to let go of just a few acres for much-needed housing and industrial expansion. But its family land, they're always quick to point out. And their ancestors would turn over in their graves if title to the precious soil was ever transferred to "others." So, the movers and shakers who work tirelessly to spur the city's economy forward make the best of the approximately four square miles that house its retail district, school system, industrial park, and residential neighborhoods.

Even the welcome signs at the town's edges have testified through the years to a crawl of growth. In the early seventies, the city's population reached the four thousand mark, then climbed slowly for the next three decades. It peaked at just under forty-nine hundred in the year 2000 but then began a gradual slide, never reaching that alluring five thousand mark. But for what it lacks in size, the town more than makes up for through its people. Its residents, young and old, serve up a homespun warmth and kindness that visitors to the town rave about until they find an excuse to return for another helping.

Matt could almost smell this air of sweet hospitality as he stepped out of his truck onto the church parking lot. It was already hot. The heat and humidity made it feel more like mid-August than late spring. But despite his dislike for Southwest Arkansas summers, he stood still, breathing in the stuffy damp air, thankful for a new day, invigorated by the events of last evening.

It had been wonderful. Beneath the glow of an amber moon and a sky full of twinkling stars that had winked down their blessing, he and Carol had lingered on the back deck 'til nearly midnight, holding hands and talking. Just two people enjoying the night and basking in each other's company. But the best part had been when he had marched victoriously past the couch and down the hallway to the comfort of his own bed. And for the first time in too long, he had slept for over seven hours straight. The streak of restless nights was finally over.

After a long minute, a car horn interrupted his reflection. He dropped his keys into his jean pocket and walked toward the handicap ramp that led up to the double doors on the south side of the Sunday School wing. Reaching the entrance, he pulled on the door handle. It was locked. Trilby had to be inside. Her blue minivan sat three spaces up from where he had parked. He knocked loudly and waited.

Through the shadowed glass, he saw the petite woman emerge from the door of the office next to his and, with a pace that defied her seventy plus years, hastily make her way toward him. She turned the thumb lock and pushed the door open.

Matt stepped into the cool interior and grabbed Trilby in a bear hug. "Good morning, Miss Watson! Have I told you lately what a fine secretary you are? And a great friend to boot!"

"My, my! Aren't we in a good mood this morning?" she replied, breaking away from him with a gentle push. "Lose your keys?"

He pulled them from his pocket and dangled them in her face. "Of course, not," he said, laughing. "You're always telling me you don't get enough exercise. Just doin' what I can to help. And I meant every word I said about you bein' a good employee and an even better friend. Roses need to be passed out to people while they're livin'."

All five feet of the tiny woman seemed to shrink with suspicion. She eyed her boss, still trying to size up his sudden display of devotion. Her expression softened and she shrugged. "Well, I guess I should say 'Thank you'. But if I'm that good of an employee, how 'bout a raise to prove it?"

Matt shook his head with amusement. "I knew it. You pay somebody a compliment and they twist it into dollars and cents."

"Oh, Preacher! I was just teasing." She raised her hand and swatted toward him, then turned and walked toward her office. Surprised at her quick departure, he wondered if he had said the wrong thing. Trilby had never been one to take issue at even the lamest of comments, a trait he wished more of his church members owned.

"I'll work on it," he said, half serious and half joking.

"Sure, you will," she replied tepidly then disappeared into her office.

Matt walked into his office and eased into his chair, still intent on the exchange with Trilby. Was something up with her?

Oh, well, he thought. *I'll know soon enough.*

Two sticky notes on the desktop caught his attention. *Call Jerry when you can. Chamber coffee tomorrow at 11:00 at Steele's Pharmacy.* Matt surmised Jerry was calling to check on him after yesterday's drama. Mike Harrison, chamber of commerce director, did his best to include his pastor in as many of the chamber's social gatherings as he could.

As he picked up the phone to dial Jerry, Trilby appeared in his doorway. She appeared winded and leaned against the door jamb. He placed the phone back in its cradle and reclined backward in his chair.

"You okay?" Matt asked.

Trilby nodded. "Can I come in?"

"Sure," he replied, his hand beckoning her forward.

Her age was fast catching up with her. That was evident in Trilby's measured steps across the room and the creases under her eyes and down her neck. But for seventy-two years old, she was still feisty and could hold her own if provoked. Her sudden geriatric look, coupled with her earlier out-of-sync conduct, made him wonder if she was about to give him a two-week notice.

She settled into one of the chairs facing him. He leaned forward, planted his elbows firmly on his desk, and clasped his hands together. Before he could speak, Trilby answered the question hanging inside his head.

"No, I'm not retiring."

Inwardly, Matt breathed a sigh of relief. Outwardly, his obvious annoyance at her ability to read his mind put a grin on Trilby's face. It was like a sixth sense she had developed over the years. And it rankled Matt to no end. Still, he was thrilled she would be sticking around.

"Well, I'm certainly glad to hear that. But I wouldn't let you even if you wanted to. We're a team in case you've forgotten. And like I told you when I got here, the younger mule, not the old one, breaks yoke first."

"Yeah, I remember, "Trilby replied. "Truth is, I couldn't leave if I wanted to. You'd be lost without me. The Good Lord only knows what a shape this place would get in. And he'd hold ME accountable for it."

The two laughed together. And despite the humor of her remark, Matt realized just how true it was. He would be lost without her. She had been here since he arrived and had been as much like a mother to him as she had an assistant. They had seen each other through good times and bad. And there would certainly be more of both to come.

"Actually, I just want to know you're okay." Her tone had turned less jovial, and her eyes were now squarely fixed on his. He realized it wasn't the time to mince words.

"I'm getting there, Trilby." He paused and looked away for a second. Her stare could be so compelling, intimidating almost. Still, he appreciated her concern and felt that in this moment of one-on-one, she deserved no less than the truth.

"The last year's been hard. On both of us. But last night we talked. Way into the night. And a lot of the bitterness between us seems to be gone. Or I think it is."

Trilby shifted in her seat. Her eyes softened. "You're my pastor, Matt. And you're my boss. But you're like the son I never had, too. It's hurt me to watch you struggle all these months. And yesterday, listening to you bare your soul in front of the whole church, seeing you pass out, and then watching you and Carol fake it at the reception....it was about more than I could stand."

A tear crept down her cheek. She quickly wiped it away with her index finger and resumed.

"I shouldn't have reacted the way I did while ago. But when you walked in and gave me that hug, it was like you were still puttin' on a front to cover up your hurt. I'm sorry."

Matt felt a lump forming in his throat. He vowed silently not to let this tender exchange turn into a cryfest. It was a new day. And a new start.

"Well, I have to admit I was a little overboard with the hug and all when I came in. But I meant what I said about you. And I do feel good about me and Carol. I think we've turned a corner."

Trilby sighed and placed her hand across her chest as if calming her heart. "I'm so happy to hear that. Why don't we celebrate? Let me take you out for lunch. Maybe we'll start a rumor about the preacher and an older woman."

Matt chuckled. "I wish I could, but I have to be at the school at 11:30. I'm eating there and speaking to the football team. Tiger fever's already started, you know."

"Oh, yes," Trilby said, rising from her chair. "Once fall gets here, that's all this town'll have on its mind."

In his head Matt agreed. The love of football by many in the town had reached an unhealthy level. And it bothered him. Thankfully, Brett was team captain this year. And Matt took comfort in knowing that his godson would use his position of influence to do what he could to keep football in its rightful second place—behind God.

Trilby walked across the room. She stopped to stare at the picture of Jesus on the wall. Ever since he had hung it there, the Head of Christ had intrigued Trilby as much as it had him. And it had led to many in-depth discussions between them about Jesus.

She walked back toward him and stood behind the chair she had just left. Her hands gripped the top of the chair back and, once again, her eyes fixed on his.

"Matt, I wanna say one more thing," Trilby said, her voice as firm as he had ever heard. "Henry and I were married nearly forty-eight years. We had our ups and downs like every married couple does. But there was one thing we always vowed never to do. And we learned it the hard way not long after we married. Neither of us ever kept anything from the other one, no matter how little or petty it seemed."

A heavy silence hung in the air as she allowed her words to sink in. Then, before walking out the door, she left him with a pointer that would leave him pondering.

"Don't ever keep anything from Carol."

He had always admired his secretary's good and wise heart. And her knack for saying the right thing at the right time over their twenty years together had always been downright uncanny and, in the end, comforting.

So, why did he suddenly feel shaken by her parting words?

CHAPTER EIGHT

Monday Morning, 11:35 A.M.

"How's your head?"

Jerry's booming bass voice sounded as loud coming through the phone as if his head deacon was sitting feet away in the passenger's seat. Matt backed the phone away from his ear as he pressed the brake and rolled to a stop at the intersection of Fifth Street and Stadium Drive.

"Well, there's still a lump back there if that's what you're talking about." He let go of the steering wheel to massage behind his left ear and flinched, more from the recollection of how the bump had gotten there than from the twinge of soreness that remained.

"So, I can do what I've been wantin' to do for twenty years?"

Matt frowned as he tried to figure out where Jerry was going with such a cryptic question. Something told him a light-hearted revelation in the form of a punch line was coming.

"And that would be?" he asked as he turned left onto Stadium Drive.

"Call you Knothead," Jerry said, his belly laugh echoing in Matt's ear.

The phone beeped low battery. "That's a good one, Deke." He hadn't found as much humor in the remark as Jerry had, but he felt smug knowing his defacto boss was likely now scowling at being called the one title Matt knew he despised.

Jerry chuckled and his tone grew sober. "All right, we're even. Seriously, you okay?"

"I'll make it," Matt replied. "You know that fall hurt my pride more than it hurt my head." He paused as Proverbs 29:23 rattled through his head. "It's kinda funny. The Bible says 'A man's pride brings him low.' I don't know if it was pride, but something sure took me down."

Jerry was quick to counter. "Come on, Preacher. Don't be so hard on yourself. You've been through a lot. The Man upstairs knows that, and He understands."

He treasured his head deacon. Jerry Mitchell was a man of spotless character, a true warrior for the Kingdom. And he always had his pastor's back.

"You always know what to say to make me feel better, Jerry. Thanks for always bein' there."

He turned off Stadium Drive onto the narrow path that led up to the Asheville High School administration building. Once again, his phone beeped, and he saw he had less than ten percent power.

"I've gotta go. I'm here at the school to speak to the football team."

"Well, pump 'em up. The whole town's expectin' another state championship this year."

"Later," Matt said, ending the call. "I hope nobody needs me," he said aloud. Seldom did he forget to charge his phone before going to bed.

He parked in one of the visitor spaces outside the admin building and got out. The sound of whistles and pigskin action could be heard in the distance. Earlier than normal practice because of the heat, Matt surmised. Though he had a stellar record on the field, winning wasn't everything to Bobby Dalton. His concern for his players' academic and physical well-being was always first and foremost. An attribute that endeared him to all but a smidgen of the town's residents. A select few who thought victories should come at any cost.

In the front office behind the counter sat Millie Rogers, a chunky middle-aged woman with thick, jaw-length red hair and make-up layers on top of layers. She smiled and greeted Matt excitedly in her loud and southern drawl.

"Hi, Matt! Good to see ya. Here to talk to the boys, are ya?"

He tried not to stare at the rainbow of colors painted on her lips, above her eyes, and down her cheeks. He looked down, pretending to brush off his trousers, then looked up and returned her good-natured welcome.

"Nice to see you too, Millie. Hope you and your family are doing well."

"Oh, we're all good. The kids are doing great at college. Aaand...." She grinned and raised her eyebrows, accenting the purple eye shadow Matt thought surely had to be pasted on. "Mark got a promotion and a raise last week!"

"That's wonderful, Millie," Matt replied. "Sounds like everything's going right for you all."

Her phone buzzed. "Superintendent's office." After a brief pause, she nodded. "I'll send him on down."

She placed the receiver back in its cradle. "Coach is waitin' for you at the fieldhouse. Says he's got your lunch ready."

"Thank you, Millie. For all you do for our school. Tell your family 'hello' for me."

She grinned and winked. "I will. And...Go Tigers!"

Kip needed attention.

Namesake of **K**endall "**K**enny" **I**saac **P**hillips, the most celebrated gridiron player in Asheville's storied history, the ferocious feline had stood vigil at the entrance to Tiger Stadium for over four decades. Now, thanks to time and the elements, the orange and black mascot, crouched low on a grey jagged boulder, was showing his age. Flaked off paint and built-up grime in the crevices of his paws and joints had tarnished his once sleek and shiny façade. And one of his upper fangs had broken off at its lowest point, leaving a noticeable imperfection in his esteemed growl. But all this loss of shine hadn't affected his ability to intimidate opponents year in and year out. Since the turn of the century, the Tigers had logged sixty-two wins versus five disappointing and often mystifying defeats. Kip had definitely done his part through the years.

Matt stroked the great beast under his chin and could almost feel a silent energy pulse forth. He paused and stared into the cat's dark, penetrating eyes. Kip was resting, quietly renewing his strength for the upcoming season. When all of Asheville would gather in the bleachers just beyond the chain-link fence to his right to cheer on their revered boys of fall.

Matt descended the sidewalk to the field house where he found the door standing open. Inside, Bobby Dalton sat slumped behind a battered wooden desk that looked like it could have fallen out of a moving truck. The room was cluttered with football paraphernalia and reeked of cigarette smoke. On the desk sat two large fold-over Styrofoam containers, two smaller ones, and two cans of soda.

"Hey, Preacher!"

Bobby's voice was loud like Jerry's but not quite as ear-splitting. Matt blinked as acrid smoke burned his eyes. He watched as the fifty-five-year-old pushed back in his swivel chair and made his way around to greet his guest up close. Agile for his age and in excellent physical condition, he was in his usual get-up—black athletic shorts, orange pull-over shirt, and a matching orange and black baseball cap that hid what little hair he had left. But what stood out was his footwear. Blue velcro sandals with dark brown dress socks—a fashion statement Matt knew would cause Bobby's wife Helen to cringe with embarrassment, considering her always pristine appearance. But the well-liked coach was a no frills kinda guy with contrasting nuances. Bland on the outside but multi-layered and intriguing underneath.

"Good morning, Coach!" Matt checked his watch. "Just barely."

The two shook hands and joined in a man hug with hard back slapping. As he backed away from the embrace, Matt felt a stinging pain where Bobby's state championship ring from last season had dug into the skin of his middle finger.

"You've still got that vice grip, Brother," Matt said, flailing his hand. "Ever broke anybody's hand?"

Bobby grinned and slapped Matt gently on the outside of his shoulder. "You're too soft, Preacher. Come on out to my farm this weekend and I'll let you drive some fence posts."

"No thank you." Matt extended his arms with his palms up. "These hands fit a Bible, not a post driver."

Bobby chortled and shook his head. "Let's eat."

The pair made their way to the two ramshackle chairs facing the front of the desk and sat down. Opening his lunch plate, Matt discovered chicken spaghetti slathered with cheese, green beans with onion, a green salad of lettuce, cucumber and sliced tomato, and a flat dinner roll. Prodded by his sweet tooth, he grabbed the smaller plate and pushed back on its top to look inside. Pecan pie with a dollop of whipped cream. His elevated cholesterol and triglycerides were about to inch a notch higher.

"So, what are you gonna talk to the team about?" Bobby asked as he tore open a tiny package of salt and sprinkled its contents over his lunch. "Gonna give 'em a little inspiration to go with their perspiration?"

Matt gripped the can of soda and popped it open. "Just a few words of wisdom and a big dose of pep!"

Bobby removed his cap and placed it reverently against his chest as Matt stabbed a duo of green beans with his plastic fork. The gesture gave Matt pause, and he looked up, surprised at how his friend's head had smoothed over since the last time he had seen him uncovered. Then, he flushed slightly as he realized the coach had just had to remind the preacher to say grace.

"May I?" Bobby asked.

"Sure," Matt replied.

The two bowed as Bobby sincerely and in a childlike manner called on the Lord to thank Him for food to eat and His many other blessings. The words warmed Matt's heart and he smiled inside. For the first time in what seemed like forever, a day had started out nicely and seemed to be getting better by the minute!

Brett Stevens was the whole package and then some. And Matt had never been more awed by his youth leader than when the charismatic and All-American teen had introduced his pastor moments earlier to the football team. His winning looks, his magnetic way with words, and his ability to attach faith to a worldly sport had all but made his pastor's ten-minute devotion redundant. But that was okay. Just being able to witness his godson in action and see the admiration for him on the faces of his peers had made the trip worthwhile. He could hardly wait to tell Brett how proud of him he was.

Matt was halfway between the field house and his truck when he heard a female voice yell his name. He looked up and saw Millie running toward him waving frantically. As he broke into a jog, her words stopped him in his tracks.

"Trilby just called. You need to get to the hospital!"

Miss Violet, he immediately thought. His oldest church member. Independent to a fault, the ninety-eight-year-old had grown wobbly over the past few months and had stubbornly refused to use a cane or walker. *She's fallen!*

He resumed his jog and closed the distance between him and Millie. When the two finally drew close, he reached out and grabbed her hand. She stood breathless, coughing heavily, her other hand patting her chest. Then, seeing up close the look of urgency coloring her face, he knew this was something more than a broken bone or a fall. When she was finally able to speak, Mille confirmed his hunch.

"It's Carol."

CHAPTER NINE

Monday Afternoon, 12:33 P.M

With his head spinning and his gut churning, Matt struggled to keep his F-150 between the shoulder and the centerline. He passed five vehicles, his horn honking and hazard lights flashing. Finally, he reached the junction of Old Dixon and Highway 178.

Seeing no vehicles approaching from either direction, he ran the stop sign and turned left into the southbound lane. In the distance Ward Medical Center sat atop a hill. The sight of it stoked the fires of his anguish as one possibility after another rushed through his mind. Stroke? Heart attack? An accident? Then, a thought that made him clutch the side of his head like a bullet had grazed it. Would he find her alive?

Expelling that notion from his head, he felt a crunching vibration. Both right tires had veered off the asphalt onto sparse gravel. He gripped the steering wheel and jerked the truck back onto the pavement. A dark-colored sedan entered the highway a short distance in front him. He hit his brake hard, laid on his horn, and passed the car on a double yellow line. Charging directly at him in the same lane was a white van, its own horn blaring. Seconds before metal hit metal, the van wheeled onto the shoulder and sped past him in the opposite direction. In his rearview mirror, the vehicle negotiated back into the northbound lane and the driver's fist shot out the window, its middle finger conspicuously extended.

Maneuvering back into the southbound lane, he breathed a silent prayer for the Hand that had just saved him from catastrophe. Then his mind was back to Carol.

Dear God, this can't be happening! All we've been through and now more!

When his truck finally lurched to a stop outside the emergency room entrance, Trilby was waiting under the covered walkway that led up to the building. He watched as her right hand dangled her eyeglasses back and forth in a rhythmic motion. That was a habit when she was mad or sad or even happy, and it told him nothing.

He hurried out of the truck and rushed toward her. She put her glasses on and reached for him, her arms trembling. He grabbed her and pulled her to him in a reassuring hug.

"I tried to call you, but you didn't answer." She pulled back from him and sighed deeply. "She's with Linda and a doctor. Jack found her outside on the driveway and called for help. He's not sure what happened."

They hurried through the automatic door. In the ER waiting room, Jack Richardson, a widower in his eighties who lived across the street from the parsonage, sat slumped and shaken. His face clenched with worry, the old man looked up at Matt and Trilby and broke into sobs. Matt walked over to him and knelt and circled Jack's hands with his.

"It's okay, Mr. Jack. I know you did all you could." He had to ask. "Any idea what happened?"

Jack shook his head from side to side. Then, he placed his index finger against his head just above his left temple. "She was bleeding right here. I tried to talk to her, but she blacked out. Thank God I had my phone with me. I called 9-1-1."

The door to the ER opened and Linda stepped into the waiting room. As he stood up, Matt felt Trilby link arms with him. Jack struggled to his feet and clutched Matt's other arm in as much a balancing act as a show of support.

"How is she, Linda?" Matt asked.

"She's stable. She took a bad blow to the side of her head. And she has a concussion. Dr. Evans, our third-year resident, just finished bandaging her up. He's with her."

"Take me to her," he demanded, loosening himself from Trilby and Jack's grip.

"Sure," Linda replied.

She led Matt into the inner sanctum of the emergency room. When they reached the cubicle where Carol lay, Linda stopped him.

"She'll be groggy and may not say much. The doctor gave her something to help her sleep. It's probably taking effect by now."

She pulled back the privacy curtain, and the two of them entered the dimly lit nook. By the gurney stood a youthful-looking guy in a white coat who looked to be no more than mid-twenties. His curly brown hair and boyish features caused Matt to ponder just how much the young man knew about doctorin'.

Matt walked to his wife's side. Seeing her at rest, watching the peaceful rise and fall of her chest, relieved him somewhat. But the brash and ugly bandage hugging the side of her head just over her left ear sent a chill through him. Her beauty had never been compromised. Now, a nasty head wound and a hideous laceration across her lower jaw had scarred that beauty.

He bent over and lightly kissed Carol's warm lips. She groaned and stirred then grew still again. He stroked her hair behind the wound and whispered 'I love you' in her ear. She stirred again and turned her head toward him as if acknowledging his words.

"She'll sleep for a while," Dr. Evans said. "I'd like to keep her overnight for observation. She should be fine in a few days, but I'd rather be safe than sorry. By the way, I'm Neil Evans."

Matt righted himself and reached across the gurney. "Matt McDonald. It's a pleasure to meet you. Though I'd have chosen different circumstances."

"I understand," Dr. Evans replied with a slight chuckle. "This is sure not the way you want to meet new people." His tone turned upbeat. "Ms. Stevens tells me she and your wife are best friends." He nodded toward Linda. "That's a mighty good friend to have. And she's an excellent nurse, too."

"I won't argue either point," Matt said. "She's been there for us a lot."

Enough small talk.

"Dr. Evans, was Carol able to say anything when they brought her in? Anything at all about how she got hurt?"

The doctor frowned and looked at his patient. "She was barely conscious. But one of the EMT's told me she kept mumbling what sounded like the word 'ladder'."

Matt stared at Linda. He knew she was thinking the same thing he was. Carol hated ladders—and heights. In all their married years, he had never known her to even get near a ladder, much less climb one. That paramedic must've heard wrong, he told himself.

Matt looked back at Dr. Evans. "That doesn't make any sense, Doc. And you'd understand if you knew my wife."

Linda chimed in. "Matt's right. It couldn't have been anything to do with a ladder. She's scared to death of 'em."

Dr. Evans shrugged and placed his hands in his coat pockets. "Where did this happen?"

"My neighbor across the street found her in our driveway. Said he couldn't tell what happened or where."

"Well, I'll bet when you get home, you'll figure it out. Let's just be thankful it wasn't any worse. Where her head hit, she could have suffered severe head trauma."

Matt leaned down and kissed Carol on the forehead. "Just rest, Sweetness. I'll be back in a little while," he whispered.

He walked around the gurney and shook Dr. Evans hand a second time. "Thank you for all you've done, Doc. I know you'll take good care of her."

"Glad to help. We'll get her to a room shortly. Right now, she needs rest—and quiet."

Matt turned and walked out of the cubicle. Linda followed him to the waiting room where they found Trilby pacing nervously and Jack gone.

"She's gonna be okay, Trilby. They're gonna move her to a room and watch her overnight."

"Thank God!" Trilby said, flinging her arms around him. "I was fearin' the worst. Like I always do."

He glanced around the room. "Where's Jack? Is he okay? He seemed pretty shook up when we got here."

Trilby pulled back and heaved a loud sigh. "I told him to go home. He missed his noon medicine and was startin' to get shaky. I just called him. He made it home okay."

Linda interrupted. "I'm here 'til eleven, Matt. There's not a lot goin' on today, so I can check in on her every few minutes. Get her admitted, then go home and see if you can figure out what happened."

"I'll be back in an hour or two," Matt said, placing his arm around Trilby's shoulders. The two exited through the automatic door they had passed through earlier. When they reached his truck, Matt leaned against it and rested his arms on the hood. He stared at the distant row of tall pines lining the property's south border.

"I don't know how much more I can take, Trilby." His hands fisted and pounded lightly on the painted metal. "Just when it looks like things are turning around, another crisis."

He closed his eyes and lowered his head. Trilby couldn't decide if he was praying silently or stifling a surge of emotion. Knowing him like she did, she was sure it was one of the two.

"Is God testing me?"

She leaned against his shoulder and patted his forearm. The words of Solomon rolled through her head then spilled off her tongue. "My son, do not despise the Lord's discipline and do not resent his rebuke. Proverbs 3, verse 11."

Again, he stared into the tree-lined yonder, allowing her sage wisdom to examine his searching heart. A long minute passed. "Is that a yes?" he asked softly.

Her reply gave his heart a thump. "I have a feeling you'll find out soon enough."

With that, she turned and walked to her minivan. As she drove out of sight, Matt opened the door to his truck and settled in behind the wheel. He sat pensively, further digesting her words. Had her last comment been idle speculation? Or was God speaking through Trilby? Foretelling of more heartache to come?

He drove around the building and parked in the lot outside the front of the hospital. As he walked the few steps to the entrance, Matt couldn't stop thinking about what the paramedic had told Dr. Evans. His eight-foot wooden ladder was heavy and bulky. Even if she had wanted to, Carol lacked the strength to hoist it up over the metal supports that held it against the carport wall. No way, he reasoned once again.

The automatic double doors opened wide, and he passed through the glass vestibule into the lobby. Cool and refreshing air invaded his nostrils and he stopped to inhale its freshness. Then, on his way to the admission's office, he prayed silently, giving thanks to the Lord for saving Carol from what could have been a life-threatening, even life-ending, mishap.

Just a scary glitch on their journey back to peace and happiness. That's all this accident had been, he told himself. She would be home soon. And the two of them would pick up where they had left off last night.

The thought warmed his insides and he smiled. When he arrived home minutes later, he wouldn't be smiling.

CHAPTER TEN

Monday Afternoon, 2:25 P.M.

Just looking at it made Matt's blood run cold.

Sitting in his driveway with the truck window down, he stared at his wife's spilled blood seized to the smooth concrete, dried and fading in the hot sun, silent testimony to what had happened inside.

Suddenly, he frowned as he pondered the bigger scene. The rust-colored droplets leading away from the central pool trailed into the carport on the passenger side of her van. *Strange*, he thought. When she had exited the house, she would have dripped blood along the driver's side and out onto the driveway. That meant what had happened had to have taken place in the carport. He glanced at the empty bay where he parked his truck. No sign of anything amiss. His eight-foot ladder hung on the back wall in its assigned place, smugly proclaiming its innocence.

He shifted into drive and inched forward until he could see in front of the van. Lying on its side between the front of the van and the built-in storage cabinets was a three-rung step ladder. And dangling loosely from the top of the cabinet was a nylon rope. One of the ropes attached to the seat of the swing. The swing he had pulled from the dumpster just yesterday afternoon and stashed high enough where he had told himself there was no way she could reach it!

Matt slammed his foot on the truck's brake. He jerked the gearshift upward into park and yanked the key from the ignition. Waves of anger swelled within him. Betrayal. The word throbbed inside his head till he felt like it would explode. His mind raced back to last night. When lying in bed they had talked about the swing. When she had agreed so willingly it would be forbidden until its sway over her was gone. And that would be his call. He would decide when or if she would ever touch it again.

Had it all been a ruse? Her sudden warming to him when he had arrived home yesterday? The coziness they had shared under the star-filled sky last night? The coffee in bed she had brought him just this morning? Yes, it had. She had buttered him up, waiting for the right opportunity to get her hands back on it—that mindless contraption he had been stupid enough to go and free from the clutches of a stinky pile of trash!

He leaned forward, planted his elbows on the lower arc of the steering wheel, and framed his face inside his hands.

I'm imagining this, he told himself.

He clenched his eyes shut for ten seconds, fifteen seconds, thirty seconds, telling himself when he opened them, he wouldn't see what he thought he had just seen. He waited another twenty seconds, thirty seconds. Then, he leaned upright and glanced toward the cabinet. The scene hadn't changed. The rope still hung there. Silent and spiteful.

The sound that erupted from inside him was half scream and half wail. It ricocheted through the truck and stung his eardrums so hard he covered them with his hands. He looked up, searching, yearning for solace from somewhere or Someone, but all he saw was the cab's beige-colored upholstery inches from his face.

"Why God?" he whispered.

Like a zombie, he opened the door and stepped out of the truck. His legs wobbled under him, and he grabbed the side mirror and steadied himself. Exhaust fumes hung in the air, and he struggled to breathe.

Water! I need water!

Slowly, he made his way past the van and into the kitchen. He grabbed a container of bottled water from the fridge and guzzled it down as he stared out the kitchen window. How could something that had once brought so much joy to his home become so vile? There was something sinister about it. It was alive, out to destroy his life. And it had to be stopped!

He placed both hands around the empty bottle and twisted until the plastic split in two. Beastly adrenalin shot through him. He tossed the bottle into the sink. Then, he turned and walked hastily out to the carport.

The ladder was a senseless intruder, a tool in cahoots with the swing. Matt stared down at it lying boldly in front of him. He had never seen it before. Where had it come from? With a quick thrust of his leg, he sent it skidding across the concrete. Then, he turned his attention to the rope hanging just inches from his face. It was frayed and dirty and being that close to it made his insides lurch. He grabbed it with both hands and pulled violently. The swing's seat tumbled helplessly down and landed at his feet.

A sly grin spread across Matt's face. Yesterday, in round one, this same foe had taken him to the ground with it. Round two would be different. Much different.

Pulling the swing behind him, he marched around the house to the back yard. As he made his way to the oak tree, thoughts of his near miss with the van barely an hour earlier filled his head. He had endangered not only his own life but the van's guiltless occupants as well. All because of Carol's selfishness.

Standing barely arm's length from the giant oak's trunk, he gazed up at the monstrous bough that had once held the swing. Despite its immense size, the branch was noticeably sagged now from the tug it had undergone through the years. He drew the swing upward and held it horizontally in his hands. Suddenly, he found himself again whisked back in time. To when girlie laughs and squeals had made this spot of ground special and hallowed. Even now, he could hear her pleading voice.

"Higher, Daddy! Higher and faster!"

It was all so vivid in his mind. Her black curls swaying in the breeze, her tiny hands clutching the ropes, her upper body reclining, and her legs extended upward to help the swing reach maximum height. Back and forth, back and forth until his arms ached and his hands tingled. But the joy it had brought to his Angel had made it all worth it.

WHACK!

In a fit of anger, he slammed the board against the tree. It splintered into two pieces that clung stubbornly together. He flipped the injured wood over in his hands and banged it against the tree again. This time, the board separated, half of it remaining in his clutch, the other half hurtling past the tree's trunk and into the chain-link fence feet away before tumbling to the ground below.

Pulling the two boards by the ropes, he walked to the leaf barrel in the far corner of the yard. The hinged metal screen on top of the barrel was steaming, too hot to touch. He wrapped the ropes around the boards, then lifted the edge of the screen by the boards' edge and pushed. The contraption met the bottom of the barrel with a loud *CLATTER!*

It wasn't enough. The enemy had been severed and degraded. But it still possessed substance and threat power. There was only one way to destroy it.

He fetched a box of matches and a bottle of lighter fluid from the back patio. After emptying the nearly full bottle of accelerant into the barrel, he tossed it on the ground behind him. Then his trembling fingers pushed back the box's cover, fished out a lone match, and slid the cardboard cover back in place.

Keeping back a safe distance, he extended his arm close enough to toss the lit match through the checkered metal screen and into the barrel. It landed on top, reluctant to drop through. Then, seconds later, like it had been tilted by an invisible energy, it plunged to the bottom. A cloud of fire and heat exploded from inside the barrel, driving him backward, his hands shielding his face.

Flames licked at the barrel's rim as thick black smoke billowed skyward. The scene was satisfying but laced with a measure of regret at the same time. The swing and its mysterious clout would soon be reduced to a pile of ashes. He watched until the flames were hidden, and the smoke was thin and pale grey. Then, emotionally spent, he trudged across the yard and into the den.

Sitting in his La-Z-Boy after a quick shower, he checked his cell phone. Nine missed calls, five voicemails, and eight texts, all of which would go unanswered for now.

Through the glass patio door, the barrel now barely smoldered. Staring at it, a sense of loneliness unlike any he had ever felt washed over Matt. Right now, he felt like it was him against the world and the world had the upper hand.

He needed to talk to somebody who would help him fight this battle. And, he could think of only one person he was willing to enlist.

CHAPTER ELEVEN

Monday Afternoon, 3:40 P.M

Chuck opened his eyes and stared at the living room ceiling. The air around him felt dank and reeked of an unsavory smell. From the kitchen, the pot of cabbage he had placed on the stove earlier hissed a rhythmic popping sound. He sat up and rubbed his eyes. How long had he been asleep? Obviously long enough for the cabbage to let go of its distinct and nasty odor.

Across the room, the box fan on the Bombay chest hummed monotonously. Its battle with the hot air streaming in through the open front door had been waging for a week now. From the back pocket of his trousers, he pulled out his handkerchief, still damp with sweat from his morning trip to the garden. He dabbed his face and neck as he looked around at his castle. It was plain and humble, devoid of modern comfort. Ever since that day twenty some odd years ago when the old attic unit had belched a loud **BOOM** and given up the ghost.

He stood to his feet. The breeze from the fan caressed his face and he breathed in its freshness. But the cool air did little to stave off the fatigue that had been plaguing him for weeks. Grudgingly, his hand circled the top of the walking cane leaning against the end of the sofa. Just this morning he had pulled it from his bedroom closet—the same cane he had put away on his forty-fifth birthday and vowed never to use again.

He trudged to the kitchen and made his way to the stove. Leaning forward, he gazed eagerly into the pot at the fresh cabbage. Its pungent aroma stung his nostrils and he recoiled. How could something that tasted so good smell so bad? It was a mystery, one he had pondered all his life and still hadn't figured out. He laid the cane on the countertop next to the stove. Then, using two dish towels hanging on the handle of the oven door, he grabbed the pot by its handles and moved it toward one of the back burners.

Suddenly, a voice pierced the musty air. "Hey, Brother."

Startled, Chuck dropped the pot onto the burner so hard a good portion of the boiling water sloshed over the side. He turned to see his pastor standing in the doorway.

"Sorry. I didn't mean to scare you," Matt said.

Chuck wiped the spilled liquid from the stovetop and turned the lit burner off. He dried his hands then draped both towels back over the handle.

"Well, I'd be lyin' if I said you didn't. Guess that's what I get for leavin' the front door open."

"What happened to the screen door?"

"I took it off last month. The screen was tore in three places. And the bottom hinge squeaked so bad it got on my last nerve."

Matt nodded in the direction of the steaming cabbage. His face twisted into a look of disgust. "I hope that tastes better than it smells."

Chuck grinned. "Ain't nothin' better than good ole boiled cabbage, Preacher."

"Do you have to hold your breath while you eat it?"

"I'll let you find out if you wanna try it. How 'bout some?"

"No thank you," Matt replied. "The smell's enough."

Despite their light-hearted banter, Chuck knew from the look on Matt's face he was preoccupied and wanted to talk. He had seen it many times. A half smile veiled by an unseen shadow.

"Have a seat," he said, pointing toward the living room.

He grabbed his cane and followed Matt to the couch. "This heat's gettin' to me, Pastor. Got a little too hot in the garden this mornin'."

He smiled and managed a small laugh. "I know you too well, my friend. Somethin's on your mind. Let's hear it."

"You don't look good, Buddy. You sure it's just the heat?"

Chuck coughed and rubbed his chest. "I'll be all right. Just need to cool down a bit. Now talk to me."

Matt stared at the rock fireplace. "Carol betrayed me."

Chuck folded his arms. "So, tell me about it."

He waited for a reply that didn't come. "Well, let's hear it. What's she done?" he asked again, a hint of annoyance now in his voice.

As his pastor recounted the events of the past few hours, Chuck sat in quiet reverence. When Matt finished, his reply was stern and harsh.

"What're you doin' here?"

There was taut silence as the question hung in the air. Finally, Chuck extended his hand and grasped Matt's knee. "Look at me, Preacher!"

The two locked eyes. Chuck's stare was hard, like a father's glare of disapproval at his son for misbehaving.

"I'm gonna ask you one other question, Preacher. And then I'll hold my peace." His tone had turned gentle and caring. "Have you been a perfect husband to Carol?"

Matt's face fell. Before he could utter the obvious answer, he felt his cell phone vibrate inside his shirt pocket.

Chuck released his grip on Matt's knee. "Answer it," he ordered.

Matt raised the phone to his ear. "Is everything okay?"

Chuck heard urgency in the female voice on the other end and saw Matt's eyes brighten as he said, "I'm on my way."

"You're blessed with a good wife, Preacher! Don't you *ever* forget that!" His hand motioned toward the door. "Now get to her! Tell her how much you love her. And...tell her you're sorry."

As Matt hurried out the door, Chuck smiled. Seconds later, a loud cough escaped him, and he clutched his chest in pain. As the cough stretched into a series of torso-shaking tremors, his heart thumped rapidly inside him. The truth was becoming more obvious by the day.

His time was short.

CHAPTER TWELVE

Monday Afternoon, 4:30 P.M.

Matt reached out and caressed the side of Carol's face then stroked the underside of her chin. "You've dreamed about her before, Sweetness. I have, too. That's natural when you lose someone you love."

She squeezed his hand and shook her head no. "It was more than a dream, Matt," she said, her tone firm with an insistent edge. "It was real. I was there with my Angel." Her face quivered as tears rolled down her cheeks. "Somebody else was there, too."

He leaned forward and pulled her to him. "Shhh!" he whispered. "It's okay." He rubbed her back in gentle circles. "Why don't you get some sleep? We can talk about this later."

With clenched fists, she pushed against his chest and stared at him with hurt-filled eyes. "I saw her, Matt. I was there with her."

Her arms relaxed and she reclined backward. Through closed eyes, a reminiscent smile spread across her face. And what she said next halted his breath.

"Jesus was there, too."

Once again, his hand circled hers as he struggled to mask the doubt that colored his face.

Her eyes flew open, and she gripped his hand reassuringly. "She looked so happy. And her smile—I've never seen her smile like that.

I wanted to hear her voice, but it was like there was no reason for anybody to say anything. Everything seemed just perfect the way it was."

"I believe you," Matt said, even as a pang of skepticism streaked through him.

"She's happy, Matt. I know that now. I just want to go be with her someday." She released his hand and sighed deeply. Then, a sudden and unexpected shift in dialogue.

"Are you mad at me?"

The question dazed Matt for a moment. He gathered his wits and offered a guarded reply, one that didn't totally absolve her actions.

"I was pretty upset when I got home. But I'm okay now."

She grabbed her gown and stared down at it. "There was this bright light. It seemed to be shining out from Him. I couldn't make out His face. But I knew it was Him. He was holding Angel's hand." Her body slumped slightly. "I could feel a Love like I'd never felt before. It was so......glorious!"

As hard as he tried, Matt couldn't make himself believe her. Right now, though, he wouldn't press the issue. After all, who was he to question?

"You know, Matt, you're gonna think I'm crazy. But I think this accident happened for a reason. I think God wanted me to see that Angel's with Him. That He needs her more than I do."

She stared out the window. "I never thought I'd say this, but I'm ready to put this whole nightmare behind me and move on. Will you help me?"

Could this finally be the turning point he had been waiting for? His hand again slipped into hers. As he held it firmly, its warmth seemed to melt away the deep-seated gap that had separated them for so long. Tears spilled down his own cheeks.

"Carol, I am so sorry." He raised her hand to his lips and nuzzled it lightly. "I've not been the husband I should have been through all this. Will you forgive me?"

She reached up and brushed away the dampness that had seized to his cheeks. Cupping his chin, she leaned forward and pressed her lips to his for several tender and alluring seconds. A tingling sensation shot through him. How long had it been since they had shared a kiss like this one?

She drew back and peered into his eyes. "I'll forgive you under one condition."

"What?" Matt asked curiously.

"That you forgive me first," she replied.

They both grinned and hugged each other tight. It was like a dream—touching the love of his life in this way and feeling her renewed affection for him. He wished time would somehow freeze, that they could stay in each other's arms forever, separated for eternity from the cold and harmful world that lay just outside the walls of this warm and friendly space. Or, better yet, that they could be whisked away at this very moment to live eternally with their Angel.

"I love you, Sweetness."

She kissed his forehead. "I love you too, Darling."

Thank you, God, Matt prayed silently.

CHAPTER THIRTEEN

Tuesday, June 11th, 6:20 A.M.

The rumble of a Kansas City Northern train roused Matt awake. Against his cheek, the couch's leather felt warm and comfortable. He found it amusing. Last night, the bed he had craved for so long had offered nothing but tossing and turning.

He showered, dressed hurriedly, and headed back to the hospital. Pulling into the parking lot, he noticed a light blue Chevy S-10 near the front entrance and parked next to it. Glancing through the passenger window, Matt stared at Brett's tattered NIV Bible lying on the seat next to a pair of white running shoes.

Arriving at Carol's room, he pressed his ear to the door and heard quiet on the other side. He pushed the door open. Brett, wearing an orange tank top and black athletic shorts, stood against the wall at the foot of the bed. The teen smiled broadly and stepped toward his pastor.

"I'm sorry I wasn't here yesterday" he said apologetically. "After you talked to the team, I started feeling sick." His face turned red as he realized how the words sounded. "Not at what you said. It must've been a stomach bug. I went home and went to bed. Mom called and told me what happened."

Matt grabbed his godson's hand and squeezed it tight. "We were lucky it..." The words hung in his throat. "We were blessed, not lucky. It could have been so much worse."

He turned and watched as the same doctor from yesterday applied the finishing touches to a smaller bandage than the first one. "Good morning, Reverend McDonald!" the young intern said heartily.

"Good morning to you. And please.... call me Matt."

"Sure thing," Dr. Evans replied. "Now that you've told me it's okay."

Matt pulled the curtain away from the bed and made his way to Carol's side. "Hey, Sweetness! How was your night?"

Her tired eyes answered before she ever spoke. "Lousy."

Pushing her tousled hair behind her ear, he bent down and kissed her temple. "Didn't get much sleep?"

"Not with all the racket around this place," she said, sighing.

Dr. Evans looped his stethoscope around his neck. "Well, you won't have to worry about being here another night. About an hour ago, I looked at the scan we did yesterday, and everything looked normal. We'll have you outta here shortly." He gently patted his patient's shoulder. "Just take it easy for a few days. If you notice any problem with your vision or have any dizziness, call Dr. Abernathy. I'd recommend you follow up with him within the week. Just to be safe."

Matt reached across the bed to shake Dr. Evans' hand. "Thank you, Doctor. I'll make sure she behaves." He gestured toward Brett. "You've met Linda's son, I take it?"

Dr. Evans nodded. "Not officially. But I figured out who he was when Nurse Stevens was here a minute ago." He shook Brett's hand firmly. "I'm Neil Evans. It's nice to meet you. You have a very sweet mother. And a smart one," he added.

"It's a pleasure to meet you, Dr. Evans," Brett replied. "And you read people well. My mom is definitely smart. And sweeter than you could ever imagine."

"How long will you be working at our hospital?" Matt asked.

Dr. Evans grabbed the clipboard holding Carol's medical chart off the table by her bed. "I'm here through 2015. Then, it's on to surgery residency. I wanna be a heart surgeon."

"Why don't you come visit us Sunday at Grace Fellowship Church on North Main? That is, if you hadn't already found a church home here in Asheville. You single or a family man?"

"It's just me," Dr. Evans replied. He paused, then his eyes brightened somewhat. "You know, I've been here nearly six months. And 'til now, nobody's even mentioned anything about church to me. You're the first one."

He cocked his head and smiled. "I've never been much of a church person. Now might be the time to check it out. What time does your Sunday morning service start?"

"Sunday school's at 9:30 and worship's at 10:45. And before all that, punch and cookies at 9:00 for guests and anybody else with a sweet tooth. And boy do we have some ladies who know how to bake 'em! Chocolate chip, peanut butter, sugar, macaroons. And Ms. Wilma Thomas' snickerdoodles—they'll melt in your mouth before you can even swallow 'em."

Brett chimed in. "You'd like our church, Doctor. Uncle Matt's a great leader. But he'll step on your toes every now and then when he preaches."

Dr. Evans frowned as he looked from Carol to Matt then back at Brett. "So, you all are related?"

Brett chuckled. "Not blood related. These are my godparents."

He moved around the bed and stood between Matt and Carol. "My dad was killed in a car wreck when I was two. And with my mom working long hours as a nurse, she needed help with me. So, these two..." His right hand gripped Matt's shoulder as the left one stroked Carol's arm. "They stepped in and helped raise me."

Dr. Evans grinned. "Sounds like you're one lucky young man." He paused to scribble along the bottom of the clipboard. Then he looked at Carol. "Let's get you outta here."

He walked to the door, then turned around. "Since I'm planning on being a heart surgeon, I do my best to eat healthy." A grin spread across his face. "I prefer oatmeal cookies."

Matt smiled. "See you at nine Sunday morning?"

"If I don't get called in here," Dr. Evans replied.

"Can I make an unusual request?" Matt asked.

Dr. Evans shrugged curiously. "Sure."

"Bring that thing around your neck with you. I've got a friend whose heart needs checkin' out."

Dialing stopped after the first ring. And from the curt "Grace Fellowship, How may I help you?" that spilled out of his phone, Matt sensed immediately that his secretary wasn't in a good mood.

"Seems like I've heard that tone before. Wanna tell me what's goin' on?" he asked.

"Hmph!" Trilby snorted. "There's nothing going on. But there's a whole lot of questions being asked and comments being made that makes me wanna tell some people to mind their own business. And it's some of our fine church members doing it."

"Now, Trilby," Matt chided. "When people call, just tell 'em what happened, that Carol fell and hit her head and that she's home and doin' fine."

"That's what I've been tellin' everybody!" she said. "But some of these people wanna make it out to be more than that. That you and Carol had some kind of powwow and she got hurt. That YOU hurt her! They didn't come right out and say it, but I could tell from their snippy comments that's what they're thinking."

Matt grimaced. "Trilby, when you hang up the phone, I want you to lock up and go home. And that's comin' from me as your boss, not your friend."

"I'm sure not gonna argue with that. I've got a feeling if one more person calls and says the wrong thing, I might just unload on 'em."

"I'll see you in the morning."

He tapped the red circle on his phone just as Carol emerged from the hallway. Wrapped in her pink robe, her face and neck were flushed red from a hot shower. She made her way to the La-Z-Boy and sat down, kicked up the footrest, and reclined backward.

"I made you some iced tea," Matt said. He nodded in the direction of the end table next to her chair.

"It's heavy with lemon. The way you like it."

She raised the glass to her lips and gulped down a large swig of the cold liquid. "Never thought I'd use that shower cap again," she said. "I've got a feeling my head's gonna be itching before Saturday gets here."

"Doctor's orders," Matt replied. "That cut needs several more days to heal."

She smiled and placed the glass back on its coaster. Her face grew serious, and she folded her hands together in her lap.

"I can't get over our godson, Matt. I've been so wrapped up in myself for so long I didn't see it. Then, when he was telling Dr. Evans earlier about us losing Bill and how we stepped in to help Linda, it hit me what a fine young man he's become."

Matt's mind raced back to the night the news had come. The parsonage phone blaring at an oh-dark hundred hour, its untimely ring portending of tragedy. A sobbing Linda struggling to tell how her husband had lost his battle with the alcoholic demon that had tormented him for years.

Two days later, standing casket-side at the visitation for his friend, he had made a promise to Bill Stevens, vowing silently to be the father figure in Brett's life. And now, almost eighteen years later, he took great comfort in knowing he had done all that he could to fulfill that promise.

"Bill would be so proud of him," Matt said wistfully. "And who knows what's in store for him after he graduates. One thing's for sure, though...he's bound for greatness. The way he's going now, he just might be the next Billy Graham."

Carol nodded in agreement. "For a year now, I've neglected him. But starting right now, that's changing. His senior year's coming up. And we're not gonna miss a one of his games this fall."

Matt couldn't help but chuckle inside. Aside from her fondness for board games, she had shunned sports of any kind all of her life. Now here she was, asserting her allegiance in cheering Brett on at every upcoming game, at home or away. An image formed suddenly in his head, of his reserved and dignified wife in the bleachers of Tiger Stadium, on her feet and waving her hands, yelling at an official. The idea spread a smug grin across his face.

Right now, she didn't know a run from a pass. Or a fumble from a touchdown. Or that on the football field, a sack didn't mean paper or plastic.

This is gonna be fun, he told himself.

A wee snore floated through the air. She had dozed off. He grabbed a throw from the hall closet and draped it over her, then tiptoed to the couch and lay down. Once again, the worn leather proved snug and restful.

He closed his eyes and soaked in the stillness of the moment. The room was hushed except for the gentle breathing of his Sweetness just feet away and the tick-tock of the clock down the hall. In an hour, maybe two, she would awaken, and life would regress to the real world outside and its endless turmoil. For now, though, his life was as close to perfect as he could imagine.

He didn't get to savor it for very long. Barely a minute later, he, too was fast asleep.

CHAPTER FOURTEEN

Wednesday, June 12th, 7:08 A.M.

Meet me at Deb's at 7:00 tomorrow morning.

The text had pinged his phone late last night. Now he and Jerry sat in the corner booth at Deb's Café, Asheville's brick and mortar magnet for early risin', coffee drinkers. Matt had just relayed the story of what had caused Carol's accident, including the mystery of the stepladder when suddenly, Jerry's jaw had dropped, and a baffling admission had spilled out.

"It was me. I'm the one she got that ladder from."

Matt leaned forward and rested his arms on the table. He raised his cup of coffee and took a sip, hoping somehow the lukewarm liquid would water down the truth of what he had just heard. It didn't happen.

Jerry rubbed his chin. "When I talked to you the other day, when you were headed to the school to talk to the football team, I was on my way to the farm store to pick up some supplies. I've been needing a short ladder. So, while I was in there, I grabbed that one. Then I ran by your house to see how Carol was doing."

Matt saw regret etched in the creases along Jerry's forehead. "It's not your fault, Brother," he said. "You didn't have any way of knowing what she wanted it for."

Unfazed by his pastor's kind words, Jerry continued. "When I got ready to leave, she walked outside with me. She saw the ladder in the back of my truck and asked me if she could borrow it. Said she needed it to dust off her ceiling fans."

Really!

Just when he was ready to put the swing out of his mind forever, a new and nagging angle had reared its ugly head. Carol had lured one of his closest friends into her scheme. It took a strange voice to quell the anger building inside him.

"How 'bout a warmup, Guys?"

From the corner of his eye, Matt caught sight of Deb Harper alongside him, coffee pot in hand. A short woman with a sizable girth at the waist, the late-fifties brunette wore her usual snug blue jeans and burgundy blouse covered by a white apron with a steaming hot mug etched in black across its upper portion. Her clothes reeked of fried bacon and whatever else Ms. Eunice's greasy griddle had churned out so far that morning.

Jerry forced a grin and raised his hand in a silent "no" gesture. He wiggled the cup back and forth. "I've had enough."

Deb smiled and pushed back her hair. "How 'bout you, Preacher? Need another round?"

"I'm good," Matt said. "By the way, what's the boss doin' workin' the early shift."

"My part-timer needed the morning off." Her eyes narrowed in a look of annoyance. "It's hard to find good help these days. By the way, I heard Carol's been in the hospital. Somethin' about a fall. Is she okay?"

"She's home," Matt replied. "Lost her balance climbin' a ladder and fell and hit her head. We were really blessed. It could have been a lot worse."

Deb patted Matt's left shoulder gently. "Give her my best. I'll send her a card," she said, then turned and walked away.

"She never meant to use that to clean her ceiling fans, did she?"

From Jerry's tone, Matt knew it was a rhetorical question, that his friend already knew the answer. All he could do was attempt to ease the guilt.

"I'm so sorry she used you like she did. And I promise you'll get an apology from her."

Jerry pulled his wallet from his back pocket and tossed a ten-dollar bill on the table. "Let's get outta here."

Matt grabbed the doorknob. He hesitated, took a deep breath, and walked inside.

Carol stood at the kitchen window gazing out at the back yard. At the sound of the door opening, she turned and walked slowly toward him. "Hi, Honey."

Matt's right hand clutched into a fist. His bridled voice betrayed his hidden anger. "When were you gonna tell me?" he asked.

She stared blankly at him like she was clueless to what he was asking her. He stiffened, his face flushing. "Don't tell me you don't know what I'm talking about!" he warned, his tone now raised and heated.

She drew backward, fear creeping into her eyes, the same fear he had seen Saturday night. For a split second, his thinking digressed. That heated argument had started at the mention of the swing. Now, a hundred feet away, it was a paltry pile of ash. But it was attacking his home again. Would it ever stop haunting him?

"Matt, what are you talking about?" Carol asked, her voice quaking.

A Pastor's Story

Like he had done four nights ago, he turned away and buried his face in his hands. The door he had just entered beckoned him back through it. Still, he wanted the truth.

"I'm talking about Jerry and the ladder. Did you think I wouldn't find out?"

She walked to his side and gently placed her hand over his. "I was gonna tell you tonight during supper. I guess I should have done it sooner."

"Yeah, you should have. I shouldn't have had to find out from him."

She circled his waist with her arms. "You're right. I should have told you at the hospital. But that didn't seem like the time or the place. And then it didn't seem important 'til I woke up this morning. And you were already gone."

He wrenched free of her embrace. "It didn't seem important to you that you *used* one of my closest friends? To get your hands on somethin' you promised me you'd leave alone?"

"Matt, it wasn't like that." Carol's eyes filled with hurt. "I wanted that ladder to clean the ceiling fans. And when I finished, I carried it to the garage." She broke into sobs. "I could see the swing up there. I just wanted to touch it....to feel it.... like I did when I used to swing Angel." She stared at him with pleading eyes. "You have to believe me, Matt. I promise I didn't trick Jerry into letting me have it. And what happened with the swing....it just happened. I'm sorry."

Was she telling him the truth? He wanted to believe her. He should believe her. But could he? She had broken her promise to leave the swing alone. As his mind grappled back and forth, her voice intervened.

86

"I'll call Jerry and apologize. And I'll make sure he knows I didn't trick him. I'm sure he feels terrible. He's probably thinking it's all his fault."

"He'll appreciate that," Matt said. "And the sooner you call, the better. He was pretty down when we left Deb's earlier."

A look of assent swept over her face. She clenched her robe tight around her and turned away to stare at the floor for a long and thoughtful minute. When she finally spoke, her tone was gentle but heavy.

"I need to tell you something, Matt. Or confess might be a better way to put it." She turned around while keeping her head down, then slowly looked up and met his gaze.

"I know I've not been a good wife since Angel died. I was so angry, I had to vent on somebody. And I picked the person I love the most." She reached out and took both of his hands in hers. "I'm so sorry for all I said and did to hurt you. I know our marriage has never been perfect and probably never will be. But there's one thing I'm so proud of. And I know you are, too."

A tear crept slowly down her cheek all the way to her jaw, then dropped hurriedly onto the side of Matt's thumb. He raised her hand to his and kissed it tenderly.

"What's that, Sweetness?" he asked.

"That we've always been honest with each other. That's the one thing that's kept us together. Especially for the past year. When we were here, together, but so far apart. We've always been truthful with each other. There's never been any secrets between us."

He drew her to him and hugged her close. An embrace like this one should have made him feel warm and consoled inside. Instead, a cold chill swept through him that almost took his breath away.

He longed desperately to gaze into her eyes all the way to her heart, to affirm the words she had just said and assure her that, yes, truth and transparency had brought them this far and would carry them on to a bright and promising future.

But he couldn't.

CHAPTER FIFTEEN

Saturday, June 15th, 10:44 A.M.

His headache now stretched from the middle of his forehead all the way behind his left ear. But that didn't stop the possibilities from cycling through Matt's brain like they had ever since he got the call at 9:30 last night.

Katie's left him again. If so, that would be the third time. *They're in financial trouble.* It was no secret the Mixons struggled when it came to money. *Was Tommy back on drugs?* The oldest of the four Mixon boys had hooked up with a bad crowd a couple years back and had just recently got his life back on track. *Had he relapsed?*

Charlie Mixon was Grace Fellowship's quiet and reclusive deacon, a married chicken farmer with four school-aged boys. He never bothered his pastor, even during those distressing episodes when a layman definitely should.

So, for Charlie to call late on a Friday night meant something was definitely up. While raising the phone to his ear, Matt had steeled himself inside. "Hey, Buddy! What's up?"

Charlie's response had been terse. "Not much. Carol doin' better?"

"Much better. She's lookin' forward to bein' in church on Sunday. Charlie, is somethin' wrong?"

"No. I was just wonderin' if you could come out to the farm tomorrow mornin'. I need to talk to you."

The cryptic invitation had only heightened Matt's suspicion that something really was off. Still, he hadn't pried over the phone. "What time?"

"How 'bout 11:00?"

"That'll work."

"See you then, Preacher."

"Good night, Charlie."

Now, some twelve worrisome hours later, he anxiously wondered what awaited him just a few miles ahead.

Five minutes later, he turned off Highway 108 onto the gravel road that led to Charlie's house. Situated at the base of Big Pine Ridge, the southernmost peak of the Osage Range, Mixon Farms stretched across three hundred acres and boasted four state-of-the-art breeder hen houses and five hundred head of the region's finest pure-bred angus cattle.

As he crossed the cattle guard into Mixon territory, he could vaguely remember the last time he had been on Mixon soil, but enough to notice things hadn't changed much since then. The exterior of the ranch-style house still needed a fresh coat of cedar stain. The roof lacked more shingles than it had the last time he was here, likely a result of the windstorm that had surged through the area in April a year ago. And the photina bushes lining the length of the house's front still hadn't been pruned and now covered all but tiny patches of exposed wood and window glass.

Charlie's white, jacked-up Toyota 4X4, wearing its usual dried mud around the wheel wells and up the sides of the frame, sat parked outside his tin-wrapped shop to the east of the house. As he parked alongside it, Matt mused at what was on the other side of it. A vehicle he had seen a thousand times—Jerry's white dually. And on the far side of the dually, another truck he recognized—Gabe Adams' silver dodge.

Three of his deacons inside the shop. Or were there more? His mind raced with pessimism. "This is not good," he muttered under his breath.

Before he had time to mull the options, the door to the shop swung open and Charlie stepped outside. Tanned and lank, he wore his usual short-sleeved navy coveralls, brown work boots, and a mesh back camo cap. Matt killed the engine and climbed out of the truck.

"Good mornin' Charlie."

"Mornin', Preacher. Thanks for comin'."

Charlie's voice was subdued, and his poker face did little to ease his pastor's anxiety. As the two men stepped toward each other and shook hands loosely, Matt thought he detected a slight tremor in Charlie's grip.

"I'm sorry I called so late last night. We decided it was time to get this over with. And away from church."

A heaviness filled Matt's gut. *WE. AWAY FROM CHURCH. GET THIS OVER WITH.* Put together, the words seemed to spell out two more: bad news.

Inside the shop, standing in a circle behind Charlie's John Deere cab tractor, were Jerry, Gabe, and Ed Steele, the owner of Steele's Pharmacy and Grace Fellowship's longest tenured deacon. The trio's quiet conversation halted swiftly when Matt stepped through the door.

With stone faces, they all turned toward him. Matt grinned slightly and walked forward slowly. Jerry returned a grin of his own, but it wasn't the broad and relaxed kind his pastor was used to seeing. The other two remained stoic like jurors who had just handed down a guilty verdict.

"Let's all have a seat," Jerry said, motioning toward five folding chairs placed in a semi-circle to the right of the tractor. "Take the middle chair, Preacher."

Amid awkward silence, Matt moved warily to his appointed spot and sat down. Jerry took the seat to his right, while Gabe settled immediately to his left. Ed and Charlie bookended the three.

Jerry crossed his legs and turned slightly toward his pastor. He leaned against the back of his chair and clutched his knee with his left hand. "The other three couldn't be here. Jim and Lou are out of town and Kevin got called into work early this mornin'."

Matt's eyes trained on a spot on the floor at his feet, where engine oil had left a crude and lasting stain. And suddenly he wondered if what he was about to hear would leave a similar stain on him, a blemish that would stay with him for the rest of his life.

"You got any idea why you're here, Pastor?" Ed asked.

The probing question in a different voice gave Matt's heart a jump. What had he done? His head blank, he chuckled lightly and shrugged his shoulders.

"Well, I thought the chicken farmer needed me." He bent forward and turned to make eye contact with Charlie, who quickly looked the other way.

Jerry straightened his legs and hunched forward. "As your deacon board, we've been made aware of somethin' we're not happy about."

Gabe shifted in his chair while Ed cleared his throat. Charlie removed his cap and shuffled it nervously in his lap. Jim remained as still as a statue. Jerry continued, his voice low and strained.

"We've been talking about what to do about it. And all seven of us agree that there's only one thing we *can* do about it."

A nervous bead of sweat that had budded on Matt's temple suddenly careened down the side of his face and splattered on the concrete floor. He promptly swiped his hand across his forehead to staunch any more that might follow suit. That's when Jerry let go with a raucous howling that seemed to echo off every square inch of metal and concrete in the building.

When he finally was able to contain his laughter, he grabbed his pastor by the shoulder, shook him back and forth, and hollered, "Gotcha, Preacher!"

Relief flooded Matt's insides. He leaned back in his chair and clutched the sides of his head. A swell of emotion that was half irritation and half anger rose within him. The urge to storm out of the building was overwhelming. Still, something told him there might be more to this caper. Something that just might make up for a bunch of grown men's immature foolishness.

"This was all the head deacon's idea," Gabe announced. "He pulled rank and made us all go along. All of us that felt like we could hold it together." He leaned slightly to his left as if staring behind Matt. "If you'll turn around, Preacher, you'll see what I'm talkin' about."

Matt turned toward the door to find the two out-of-town deacons and the one called in to work on Saturday staring at him. All three of them grinned from ear to ear as they moved toward him. Suddenly, he found himself surrounded by seven well-meaning pranksters whose weird sense of mischief had all but given him a stroke. Strangely though, he was suddenly overcome with a new and fierce sense of appreciation for these men. No matter their oddball brand of comedy, he knew they were all about one thing. Love for their pastor.

Jerry circled his arm around Matt's shoulder. "You can hit me if you want to, Pastor. And it'll be okay. But with all that's been goin' on in your life, we wanted to do somethin' to lighten things up a bit for you. Somethin' to make you laugh."

Lou Vincent stepped forward. Middle-aged and short, with a rotund belly and a head fast balding, his hands were clasped together behind his back in his signature pose of quiet submission. "I tried to talk 'em out of it, Pastor. But I got overruled. Don't hold it against me, okay?"

Before Matt could answer, Kevin Kimble, easily the most jocular of the group, interrupted. "Now, Preacher, don't' you believe a word of that. Lou was in on it just like the rest of us. He wanted it to go on longer than it did. When we was standin' outside the door just now, he got mad when Jerry cut it short."

Jerry moved to the center of the group. "Now, now, fellas we've had our fun. Let's get to the real reason we're here." He summoned Matt back to his side. "I think it's safe to say you've had a rough year, Pastor. You and your bride have been through more this past year than anybody should have to go through in a lifetime. I know I couldn't have handled it the way you did. And I doubt any of these other guys could've, either."

He paused to clear his throat of a lump fast forming. "We all love ya, Preacher. And here's a little somethin' from the church to let you know just how much everybody loves and appreciates all you do for us."

He reached inside the front pocket of his trousers and pulled out a white, letter-size envelope, crimped at its corners and stuffed to the point it looked ready to pop loose the scotch tape that held it together. Jerry handed the love offering to Matt and pulled his pastor to him, this time in a warm embrace. The other six deacons responded with a short round of vigorous applause.

The hug over and the applause ended, Jerry draped his arm up Matt's back and gripped his shoulder. There was a new excitement in his voice. "We're not through, Pastor. You know, I mentioned earlier we're not happy about somethin'. Ed reminded me this week that you hadn't had a raise in five years. Well, come July, you're gettin' one."

Again, applause echoed around the building. Matt stood speechless, his gratitude evidenced by a posture of silent humility. He pushed the envelope inside his jean pocket. Its bulk created a weighty feel, one that sent a thrill of excitement through him. He hugged his deacons one by one. And for the first time ever, he watched Ed Steele, a man as hard and stoical as the concrete beneath his feet, shed a lonely tear. Just one tear, but proof that even the most wooden of men can cry.

Forget the raise. Right now, he had all he needed. A room full of brothers and a pocketful of love. As he moved about the room, the bundle seemed to grow heavier as if multiplying by the minute. His fingers itched to retrieve it, to find out just how much green love his flock had blessed him with. But this was one package he dared not open before he arrived back home. For the first time ever, he and Carol were about to celebrate Christmas a full six months early!

He thanked God silently for this blessed moment. Life was good again. But, a cynic by nature, he couldn't help but wonder how long it would stay that way.

CHAPTER SIXTEEN

Sunday, June 16th, 7:14 A.M.

Matt rolled onto his back, opened his eyes, and stared at the popcorn ceiling above the bed. The smell of bacon hung in the air, and for a few brief seconds he was a child again, lured awake by the same tantalizing smell that now tickled his nostrils. The one that on many mornings long ago wafted from his momma's cast-iron skillet to his bedroom at the end of the hall. Those had been good years! The kind that only weeks ago he had decided were a thing of the past. But three days ago, things had started to change for the better.

It had all started Thursday morning when Carol called Jerry over to set things straight about the swing. Before it was over, all three of them were hugging and shedding tears of reconciliation. That had been followed by waves of laughter and light chatter over coffee and blueberry muffins brought over earlier in the morning by Eva Womack, their spinster neighbor to the east. Jerry had left with the ladder, satisfied that his innocent purchase had turned out to be a prop and not a pawn.

Matt rolled back onto his side and gazed out the window at the barrel. The swing was gone—really gone. Again, he marveled at what a journey it had taken him on. A journey filled with years of joy, then twelve long months of frustration, heartbreak, anger, and finally resolution. Reflecting back, he felt a strange measure of thanks for it. He had triumphed over it in the end. And now he felt an inner strength he hadn't felt before, one that just might help him face future giants that would rise up to challenge him.

Friday had come and gone quietly with nursing home visits in the morning and afternoon preparation for today's sermon. There had been one stab of humor along the way. He had almost finished with his notes when, without warning, Trilby had burst into his office, her cheeks cherry red with irritation.

"If that pushy salesman calls here one more time, I'm gonna let him have it! I've told him four times now we buy office supplies here in town. But he won't take no for an answer."

Matt had laughed and waved her toward the door. "Call it a day, Woman." He had no more mouthed the words when she turned and flounced out of the room in a huff, arms flailing. And an age-old question had again rattled through his head. *Will that woman ever chill out?*

He had followed her lead barely ten minutes later. As he locked the door behind him and walked to his truck, the roller coaster ride of the past week had replayed inside his head. It had definitely been anything but dull, so much so that he'd quickly sent a plea heavenward for a few days less taxing.

On the way home, he had dropped by Arnold's Pizza Shack and picked up a large, thick crust meat lover's with extra mozzarella and a side order of cheese sticks. It was a treat reminiscent of their dating days, and by the glow of a single candle, he and Carol had savored every morsel. Then, cuddled together on the couch, they had watched for the umpteenth time as George Bailey rambled contentedly through life until his bumbling Uncle Billy mislaid a wad of bills that ended up in the hands of the town tyrant.

Seeing the dastardly Mr. Potter bring kind, well-meaning George to his knees always tugged at Matt's heartstrings. And Thursday night had been no different. Every time he watched the story, he couldn't help but wonder: why hadn't the gravel-throated villain of the movie got his due in the end? But then, wasn't that the way real life often played out? Good folks suffering while the bad ones were able to hide their trickery and thrive? Even so, as Auld Lang Syne rang out while the credits rolled, he had to agree with what George learned in the end: It really was a wonderful life!

An hour after the movie wrapped, Charlie had called, setting up the events of yesterday. Those crazy, mischievous guys and their less-than-innocent prank! He smiled and dreamed of payback, how or when he wasn't sure. But the idea quickly faded. All their tomfoolery had been fueled by love and nothing more. And the proof was now tucked in the side drawer of the dining room buffet.

Arriving home yesterday, he had handed the envelope to Carol. She had handed it back. That's when, wide-eyed and expectant, they had sat at the kitchen table and tore into it together. The bills had spilled out fan-shaped. Six one-dollar bills, twenty-six fives, ninety-six tens, fifty-three twenties and forty-four Benjamins! It all added up to $6,556.00. Enough to payoff Carol's van and her only credit card. And purchase that new riding lawn mower Matt had been pining for and still have just over a thousand dollars to spare. Christmas had come early to the McDonald house!

From the kitchen the bacon sizzled and popped and sent his taste buds watering. He rose and grabbed his light-weight silk robe resting on the wooden settee by the bed, draped it around him, and creeped slowly up the hall. Carol stood at the stove, a wooden spoon in her hand, stirring in circles. He eased catlike toward her and raised his arms to circle her waist. The sudden contact startled her, and she dropped the wooden spoon onto the stovetop between the skillet and a stainless-steel saucepan.

"Good morning," he whispered gently, planting a light kiss on the nape of her neck. "I didn't mean to scare you."

"Sure, you didn't," she replied laughingly. Her hand retrieved the dropped spoon and resumed stirring. Matt peered over her shoulder and noticed a dark creamy substance clinging to it. He grinned widely as images of his childhood again sprang forth. His momma's cathead biscuits piled high on a plate beside a bowl brimming with the same delicacy now bubbling inside the pan.

Chocolate gravy! A timeless and tasty treat he had adored and craved since he was a young boy. But rarely did he get to savor it these days. His wife had become quite health-conscious in recent years, certain that sugar was a dietary nemesis that could only be consumed once in a great while. That notion had been boosted after Matt's last physical when his blood count revealed an elevated cholesterol level.

Carol grabbed the pan by the handle and moved it to the burner directly behind it. She placed the skillet with the done bacon on the other rear burner and flipped both front burners off. "I know you don't need this, Pastor. But after what you brought home yesterday, I thought we should celebrate." She turned and smacked him on the lips. "Of course, you don't have to eat it if you don't want to."

He drew her closer to him and returned a lingering kiss. "I love you, Sweetness." Her eyes flickered with a shine that had gone out after the accident. What a thrill it was to see that shine back!

A burning sensation filled Matt's nostrils. He breathed in deeply and stared at the skillet. But it wasn't bacon he smelled.

"Do you have biscuits in the oven?

Carol's eyes widened with alarm. She whirled around and pulled the oven door open. Heat and smoke plumed upward and the two of them recoiled backward. Carol fanned the air with both hands, then grabbed the oven mitt resting on the countertop. She quickly removed a cookie sheet filled with black-topped biscuits, placed it on the front of the stove, and slammed the oven door shut.

For a few seconds, the two stood motionless, neither moving. Then, they both broke into laughter and fell into each other's arms.

"We'll scrape the tops off," Matt said. "By the time they're dipped in the gravy, it'll be like they were never burned in the first place."

Minutes later, with the table set and grace said, Matt split one of the biscuits open and smothered it with gravy. He forked off a bite and eased it into his mouth. The sweet taste was satisfying like no other. By time-honored tradition, a bite of bacon between biscuits helped to keep the gravy from becoming bitterly sweet. By the time he and Carol finished eating, only two biscuits and scarcely a cup full of gravy remained. Enough for a late-night snack after the evening service.

Matt leaned back in his chair and rubbed his stomach. He reached across the table where Carol's hand rested and placed his hand over hers.

"I'm not just saying this, Sweetness, but that was as good as my momma ever made. You can surprise me with that anytime you want to."

She closed her other hand over his and rubbed it gently. Her tone was firm but in a mild and endearing way.

"I wanna keep you around for a while longer, Pastor. You still have work to do. *WE* still have work to do. And we need our health to get it done. Agreed?"

Matt nodded. "I'm with you." He leaned forward. "How 'bout I help you clear the table before I go pick up Chuck?"

A Pastor's Story

Carol turned and studied the clock above the sink. "It's a little early, isn't it?"

Matt rose and placed his dirty knife and fork in his plate. "He'll hang out in the library 'til service starts. Says that's where he does some of his best thinkin'."

Carol stood to her feet. "I can tell you're really worried about him." She grabbed her own plate and the cookie sheet with the pair of leftover biscuits. "Do you think it's anything serious?"

"I'm not sure. He's really gone down over the last few weeks. But you know how stubborn the old codger is about goin' to the doctor. Says when it's his time to go, no doctor can do anything about it."

They walked to the sink and deposited the plates and utensils. Carol inserted the stopper into the wash side and pushed the faucet up and to the left for hot water.

"He's been a true friend to you. The closest friend you've had since we've been here in Asheville." She pulled the faucet downward to stop the water and stared rigidly at her husband. "But you may have to give him up soon, Matt. Sooner than you think."

Her words tore through his chest like a knife. Had she just confirmed what he had been fearing for the past few weeks? That he was about to lose his best friend? He shook the possibility out of his head.

"I know," he said. "I'll deal with it when it happens. 'Til then, I'll see if I can talk some sense into him about going to get checked out." He stared at his watch, then grabbed her shoulders and kissed her forehead. "I've gotta go. Love you."

"Love you too, Pastor."

The drive to Chuck's house would normally have taken Matt no more than ten minutes. But today, there would be a quick detour. He parked his truck as close to the grave as he could and walked briskly to it. Since his visit last week, a bouquet of red roses had been placed in the shadow of the headstone. A caring church member most likely, Matt reasoned. He knelt and caressed the image of his child.

"Thank you, Angel, for helping your mommy. She's okay now… knowing you're happy." He choked back a tear. "I love you, Angel."

For a somber minute he tarried, then rose to his feet. As he strolled back to his truck, a weight seemed to lift from him. The darkest chapter of his life appeared to be over, and he prayed it had set the stage for a more promising one to be scripted.

Promising? Time would tell.

CHAPTER SEVENTEEN

Sunday Afternoon, 12:30 P.M.

Matt watched anxiously as the diaphragm of the stethoscope moved to and fro across the left side of his friend's chest. As he gripped the back of Chuck's trembling hand, he felt his throat thicken and his nose mist with sadness.

"Breathe out," Dr. Evans said, removing the ear tips and circling the tubing around his neck. The look on the young intern's face told a grim story.

Chuck grabbed the arm of his chair and leaned backward, staring at his pastor. "I'm plum used up, Preacher. Just walkin' from the pew back here wore me out." He exhaled and coughed loudly into his fisted hand.

"Now, hold on, Buddy. Don't go givin' up just yet." Having resigned himself to bad news, Matt's words sounded hollow in his own ears. "Let's hear what the doctor has to say."

Dr. Evans propped against the desk and freed himself from the stethoscope. He doubled the rubber tubing and held it in his hand. "The left side of your heart's barely pumping. I'm not for sure, but I think you're in the final stages of congestive heart failure. You need to see a cardiologist."

A surrender grin settled on Chuck's face, followed by words that sounded like a wise father advising his brainy but naive son.

"Listen to me, Young Man. I'll be sixty-nine years old in a month. I've had a good life. It's been hard. But the Lord's seen fit to give me years that add up to just one shy of a man's allotted time."

Chuck bowed his head. When he looked up his eyes were glazed with a mixture of longing and heartache. Seldom had Matt seen this soft side of his closest friend. And never had Chuck shared with his pastor what he revealed next.

"I lost my wife Louise and my baby boy in a fire when I was just twenty years old. I wanted to kill myself. Thought I couldn't go on. But somethin' kept tellin' me I was still here for a reason. That's when I signed up and shipped off to Vietnam."

He ran his hand along and down the outside of his left leg. "I've been shot up and got metal in me right here to show for it." His hand patted the back of his calf. "But you know what? That was so we could all be here right now and be free, and I wouldn't change that for the world."

"Mr. Wilkins, I really think---"

A raised hand and a hard stare stopped the young doctor mid-sentence. Chuck shook his head from side to side.

"First off, it's Chuck. I ain't never been a mister and don't pretend to be one now. And second, save your breath about your cardi-whoever. We'd be wastin' his time and mine."

Dr. Evans appeared perplexed by what he had just heard. He looked to Matt for support. All he got back was an eyeful of helpless annoyance.

"He's as contrary as they come, Doc," Matt said blithely. "Once he makes up his mind, there's no reasonin' with him."

Dr. Evans folded his arms and looked soberly at Chuck. "I wish you'd at least let me make a phone call for you."

Chuck twisted his lips. "Wouldn't do any good," he said meekly. "It's all up to the Man Upstairs now." His tone brightened a bit. "Who knows, I may outlive both of ya'll. Or I may go tomorrow. Either way, I'm happy."

The heaviness in the room lightened. As Matt looked on, Dr. Evans shrugged helplessly while Chuck grabbed his cane and rose to his feet, tottering briefly. He shook the young intern's hand limply then looked at Matt.

"Take me home, Preacher."

"Why didn't you tell me about your wife and son before now?" Matt asked.

Chuck groaned and pulled his bad leg inward toward the couch. His eyes grew wistful. "It's hard for me to talk about it even now. I've always blamed myself for not being home when the fire started. If I had been there, things might have turned out different. Maybe I could have saved them."

For Matt, hearing someone else express blame over the loss of their family pulled forth his own personal guilt at losing Angel. And he now felt regret at not being able, through the years, to help Chuck cope with such a devastating loss. After all, for a full year now, his best friend had done everything in his power to help ease his pastor's grief. If only he could have returned the favor.

Chuck groaned and lightly massaged his chest. "I knew what you were going through when you lost your little girl. And I felt your pain, Brother. More than you'll ever know."

Matt's throat tightened. "Ever since I got to town, you and I have shared something special, Brother. You're the best friend I've ever had."

"You're a good man, Matt. By the way, I owe you an apology. I was kinda rough on you when you were here the other day."

"How?" Matt asked, frowning.

"By what I said to you. But you were feeling sorry for yourself. And you're a bigger man than that."

Matt chuckled. "You were pretty harsh. But it's what I needed to hear."

"I take it you two worked it out. You looked like a couple a' lovebirds in church this morning."

"We're good," Matt said. "Life's slowly getting back to normal."

Chuck glanced at his watch. "Ya'll got a date for lunch?"

'We're meeting Linda and Brett at Michael's Cafe. They're probably waiting on me right now."

"Then you best get goin'," Chuck said pointing to the door. "And remember, each day's a gift, Pastor. Treasure every one of 'em."

Ordinarily, Matt would have found Chuck's words cliché. But as he drove away, he reminded himself just how pivotal they had become in his life.

End of Part Two

CHAPTER EIGHTEEN

Tuesday, September 3rd, 1:10 P.M.

Matt watched the grey, wet scene outside his office window with mixed emotions. As thankful as he was for the rain after a brutally hot and drought-filled summer, he voiced a silent prayer for it to stop. Hurricanes rarely flung moisture Asheville's way. But Hurricane Debbie had bucked that trend in a big way. Her powerful winds and blinding rains had pummeled Southwest Arkansas since late Sunday evening.

Now emergency personnel, with the help of concerned residents, were sandbagging, racing to hold back a surging Baker Creek that threatened neighborhoods on the east side of town. The city lake just north of town had inundated several structures on its south side. Gusting winds had downed numerous trees loosened by saturated ground. And at last check, the Weather Channel called for Debbie's remnants to hang around until tomorrow morning.

"Amazing, isn't it?"

Trilby's voice gave Matt a start. He glanced toward his office door and stifled a laugh. Her hair, normally immaculate and painstakingly in place, lay damp and tousled about her head, thanks to an umbrella turned inside out by the stiff wind outside.

He nodded toward the window. "I assume you mean the rain?"

Trilby shot him one of her what-else-would-I-be-talking-about looks. "Of course, that's what I mean. I sure wasn't talking about this lovely hair," she said, pushing a damp strand behind her ear. "It's a shame we can't bottle all this rain up and save it for the next dry spell."

"You're right about that," Matt said. "Have you heard how much we've got?"

"The radio station just reported a little over ten inches. And they said it's not supposed to move out 'til in the morning," she said, frowning.

Matt's phone rang. He reached to answer it, but with a wave of her hand Trilby stopped him. "That's what you pay me for," she quipped.

She walked to her office. Seconds later, his phone buzzed. "Butch Randall on line one."

Matt pressed the blinking light and hit the hands-free button. "Hey, Butch! How's my favorite athletic director?"

"Fair to middlin', Preacher" a voice replied in a distinctly upbeat and nasal tone. "Getting' geared up for kickoff and tryin' to stay dry in the process."

Butch Randall had served as the school's athletic director for over three decades. Short, rotund, and seventy-ish, he loved all sports, but high school football was his passion. And with the first game of the season just three days away, Matt could feel Butch's energy and enthusiasm resonating through the phone.

"Me too," Matt said. "We may need a boat to get to the stadium Friday night. And we may need to think about buildin' an ark if this keeps up."

Butch laughed. "I'm afraid I wouldn't be much help. I can't even drive a nail. Or push a saw."

"You and I got somethin' in common, then. Whatcha got on your mind, Buddy?" Matt asked, though he already had an inkling.

Butch cleared his throat. "I was wonderin' if you'd give the invocation Friday night. You've been doin' it at the first home game for years now. It's sorta become a tradition."

Matt's tone grew serious. "Can we still get by with it?"

"As far as I'm concerned, we can," Butch said. "I'm not about to let a few radicals rob the rest of us from acknowledgin' the Man Upstairs. Just promise me you'll go my bail if they haul me in."

"I've got your back," Matt said. "What about the field? Do you think it'll dry out enough by Friday to play on?"

"Oh, we'll play on it no matter what kinda shape it's in. I just dread patchin' it up afterwards."

"I'll be there," Matt said. "And I'll keep it short."

"Thank you, Preacher. I owe you one. Let me buy you lunch soon."

"Sounds good. See you Friday night."

"Later," Butch said. "And go Tigers!"

Matt lifted the receiver and placed it gently back in its cradle. He couldn't believe another football season had rolled around. And as they always were leading up to kickoff, expectations throughout the town were high. Sports analysts had already picked the Tigers to win their conference and vie for a state title.

The rain eased suddenly to a gentle tapping on the roof above him. He walked to the window and stared out at the ponded ground. A half-minute later, the rain surged back, smothering the glass and blurring his view. As he gazed into the silver spray, his mind raced with images of the Tigers' championship matchup last year in Little Rock against the Leopards of cross-state rival Wesley Academy.

The game had been played in sub-freezing temperatures with occasional bouts of sleet. Both teams had struggled to move the ball in the cold and slick conditions. But in the end, Brett's 110-yards rushing had carried the tigers to victory and earned the teen most valuable player honors. But as exciting as that day had been, something had been missing.

Attending games last year by himself had made for a long season. This year, Carol would be by his side. And together, they would cheer the Tigers on. The thought refreshed him, and he smiled. Then, as quickly as it came, the smile morphed into a frown of worry.

It was an exciting reality but a sobering one. The entire team, the entire town was counting on Brett to lead the Tigers back to the playoffs. That was too much pressure on a seventeen-year-old. What if he buckled under the strain? What if an injury sidelined him? What if his effort fell short?

Whatever happened, good or bad, Matt vowed silently to be there for his godson. That promise would turn out to be life changing.

CHAPTER NINETEEN

Friday, September 6th, 7:23 P.M.

A fiery sun had dipped below the treetops just enough to cast a burst of orange over the fading horizon. Through the tinted glass of his windshield, Matt squinted his eyes, scanning the back side of the home bleachers. They were packed from end to end. An overflow of fans lined the fence circling the south end of the field.

As he stepped out of his truck, a strong voice with an unmistakable lilt echoed through the stiff September air.

"Good evening, Ladies and Gentlemen, and welcome to Tiger Stadium for the Tigers' season opener against the Saints of Melrose Christian."

Asheville alum Josh Weston was beginning his twenty-ninth year as public announcer and play-by-play man. At his introduction, a loud cheer erupted from the stands, followed by chants of "TI-GERRS! TI-GERRS! TI-GERRS!"

Dodging puddles left behind by Debbie, Matt raced across the parking lot, envisioning how frantic Butch Randell had to be by now. When he reached the private entrance at the northeast corner of the stadium, he found Butch standing guard, as fidgety and nervous as he had imagined.

"I was startin' to worry you'd forgot me," Butch said, pushing open the chain-link gate.

Matt slipped through and cuffed Butch on the shoulder. The two of them scooted up the shaky flight of stairs to the rear door of the press box and rushed inside. Josh sat in the middle cubicle, voicing his final comment about a fifth quarter fellowship for students after the game. At the sound of the door, he turned, rose slightly, and motioned Matt forward.

"And now, Ladies and Gentlemen, please rise for the invocation to be given tonight by the pastor of Grace Fellowship Church, Matt McDonald. We ask that you then remain standing for our national anthem, which will be followed by the Asheville High School alma mater."

Matt settled into the vacated chair as the crowd below rose to its feet in a reverent hush. True to his word, he kept the prayer short, ending it with his trademark "Go Tigers, Go!" The tag evoked cheers from the home stand and loud boos from the visitors' stand across the way.

He hastily bid goodbye to both men and raced out the door and down the stairs. When his shoes hit dirt, the strain of 'O say, can you see' halted him in his tracks. But the melody was immediately squelched by a stinging realization. He had forgotten to do something he had never failed to do before. Pray for divine protection on the two teams about to collide on the field.

Matt panned the bleachers, searching for Carol and Linda. Finally, he spied them on the top bleacher. Clad in denim jeans and orange tee shirts with black tiger heads on the front, they looked like twinkies. Chuckling, he made his way up the steep steps toward them. Never in his wildest dreams had he imagined Carol in a rumpus scene like this.

Matt squeezed between his wife and a heavy-set woman who shot him a glare of annoyance at being displaced. He grinned and offered the woman a quick 'Sorry' just as the Tigers, wearing their black home uniforms and helmets the color of ripe pumpkins, tore through the giant banner in the south end zone.

The Tiger faithful sprang to their feet, hands clapping and feet stomping. Confetti fluttered. Band music blared. Nimble cheerleaders cartwheeled across the field. Amid the pomp, Matt watched as Brett nonchalantly made his way to the sideline, where he knelt on one knee and briefly bowed his head before being surrounded by his coach and a swarm of high-fiving teammates.

"There he is," Matt said, pointing.

Carol craned her neck. "I don't see him. What's his number?"

"Fifteen," Matt replied. "He's in the middle of those players huddled around Bobby. They're getting a last-minute pep talk from their Coach."

Carol grabbed Matt's shoulder and pulled him down to whisper in his ear. "I'm worried about Linda. Ever since I picked her up, she's been so quiet. She won't tell me what's wrong."

Matt frowned. "She's probably just sentimental about this being Brett's last year. Once the game starts, she'll be okay."

Josh's voice boomed over the loudspeaker now just feet away. "The Saints have won the toss and have elected to receive. The Tigers will kick and defend the north goal."

As the home team took the field, the fans whooped louder, urged on by the rest of the team and the bouncy cheerleaders spread out across the running track. Suddenly, the referee's whistle blew. Tiger kicker Dylan Foster approached the ball perched on the tee and, with a forward thrust of his right leg, booted the ball high into the air and down the field.

A Pastor's Story

A Saint player cradled the ball at the fifteen-yard line and raced upfield. As eleven black figures charged toward him, he slowed suddenly, gauging his position. After key blocks by two of his teammates, he zigzagged forward, then cut right and headed for the sideline. The Tigers angled in hot pursuit, but they were no match for the lanky speedster. Once he cleared the midfield stripe, all that lay in front of him was green grass and a clear path to the end zone. Seconds later, he high stepped across the goal line as the visitors' stand cheered wildly and the Tiger faithful settled despairingly onto the bleachers.

"That's sure not the way the season was supposed to start," Matt said, half chuckling. "Hope that's not a sign of things to come."

"Now Brett gets to play, right?" Carol asked, upbeat.

"Yep. Now the Tigers go on offense."

Matt stared past Carol at Linda. Her face was blank and expressionless. Like she was clueless as to what had just happened. She turned and met his gaze as a tear crept down her cheek.

"This is not right," she said.

Carol draped her arm around Linda's shoulder and swabbed the tear away with her index finger. "What do you mean, Honey? What's not right?"

Linda's head shook from side to side. "Something's just not right. I can't explain it. I just feel it."

Matt reached over and patted Linda's hand. "It's just jitters, Linda. Once Brett finds his groove and gets his running game goin', we'll be okay. This oughtta be an easy win."

It was soon obvious the game would be anything but. The Saints, hyped and well-coached, had come to play. Helped by a strong defense and two fumbles by Brett, the visitors held a 21-7 halftime lead. As the Asheville High marching band took to the field, the home fans sat in stunned silence. When the two teams returned for the start of the second half, only a fraction of Tigers fans rose in a feeble show of support for their team.

Thanks to a tipped ball, a pick six, and a successful two-point conversion, the Tigers narrowed the Saints' lead to 21-15 midway through the third quarter. Both defenses stood tall and forced three straight punts. With just over two minutes to go and the Saints trying to kill the clock, providence intervened for the Tigers when they recovered a freak fumble at the Saint 40-yard line. Bobby Dalton called his final time-out.

"This is it," Matt declared. "If we don't score here, it's over. We won't get another chance."

Carol gripped his hand nervously. "Brett looks like he's limping a little. Do you think the coach'll let him go back in?"

"I guarantee you, there's no way Bobby can keep him out of there," Matt whispered in her ear. "He's team captain. And he's not about to let his teammates down."

As the Tiger offense broke huddle and took the field, the Tiger faithful rose to their feet. *GO TIGERS GO! GO TIGERS GO! GO TIGERS GO!* The chant echoed off the metal bleachers and across the field. It was met from the opposing stand with an imploring *DEFENSE! DEFENSE! DEFENSE!* Players and coaches on both sidelines pranced and hollered feverishly. The referee blew his whistle and the clock rolled.

On first down, Brett snaked to the thirty-six-yard line for a gain of four. On second down, he surged through the Saint defense for another five yards. Then, on third down, the center snapped the ball low. It squirted through Vince Anderson's legs to the thirty-eight where the quarterback fell on it just before a Saint player covered it.

Thirty-one seconds to play. Fourth and eight. No timeouts.

Bobby Dalton signaled in the play. The game clock continued its slide. Amid the frenzy all around him, Matt watched as Brett gathered the Tiger offense in a circle. Although his body language seeped confidence, his godson couldn't mask the fatigue that slumped his shoulders and planted his hands on his hips.

The Tigers approached the line of scrimmage where the Saint defense awaited. The play clock ticked under ten seconds. After a hard count, the center snapped the ball to Vince, who retreated three steps backward. He raised the ball to fake a pass, but then handed off quickly to his star running back.

Brett secured the ball then searched for an alley. He moved between two blockers, juking first left then right until he was past the defensive line and into the secondary. A defensive back plowed toward him and lunged low for an ankle tackle. Brett went airborne and hurdled the player who landed hard on the turf, pounding his fists with frustration.

Watching from the top bleacher, Matt held his breath. If Brett could get past the safety, he would be home free. If he could fake the player out with one of his signature cuts, the end zone was his.

If.......

The scream was bloodcurdling. It rang out above the cacophony of the crowd. Its ghastly tone jolted Matt's heart and hurled Carol into his side. He braced his left leg to keep from falling then gathered her into his arms. The two stared at each other, addled momentarily. Then, the truth hit like lightning.

It was Linda.

Next to them, she stood stock-still. The scream seemed to have etched itself across her face. Her eyes were frozen, hollow and unmoving. Her cheeks were the color of chalk. Then, without warning, she slumped against Carol, unconscious, and the two of them collapsed to the bleacher.

"Honey, wake up! Wake up!"

Carol rocked her best friend back and forth, but her plea fell on deaf ears. As Matt looked on, a loud moan escaped the mass of humanity surrounding him. He looked toward the field.

Play had come to a confusing halt. Three officials crouched over a figure lying on his back with only his legs exposed. Just feet away from the shadowy scene, an inverted helmet rested direly on the turf.

At the officials' urging, two first responders hurriedly pushed a gurney onto the field from the northwest corner of the stadium. When they reached the still player, the men in black and white moved away, revealing his identity. And the blood that oozed from his mouth and his right ear.

Matt slumped to the bleacher. As sobs racked his body, Tiger Stadium fell deathly silent.

CHAPTER TWENTY

Friday Evening, 10:10 P.M.

Matt's mind raced backward. He remembered the scream and Carol falling against him. After that, it was all a blur. Whatever had happened on the field, somehow Linda had sensed it seconds before.

What had happened?

Next to him, Bobby Dalton sat slumped and dazed. His wife Helen stroked his back soothingly. Matt grabbed his friend's knee.

"Coach, I didn't see what happened."

Bobby leaned back and clutched Matt's hand. He squeezed it so hard Matt grimaced in pain.

"He tried to run the safety over, but the kid was too strong. He hit Brett hard enough that it jarred his helmet off. As he was driving Brett backward, another player..."

Bobby's upper body shook with grief. His next words sent a marrow-deep chill through Matt.

"Another player hit him from the side. His helmet crashed into the side of Brett's bare head."

Matt looked around him. The whole Tiger team, still in their black uniforms, sat stunned and distraught. And instantly Matt found himself thrust back to another dark and shadowy time, the days following Angel's death.

Dear God, don't let him die!

Suddenly, the door to the right opened and Neil Evans emerged. He stopped and studied the somber scene. Then, he drew a long breath and placed his hands into the pockets of his white coat.

Matt stepped toward the young intern and searched his eyes. They spoke an unwelcome message, one he didn't want to hear, one he felt sure if uttered would shatter the room into a million pieces.

Dr. Evans stepped past Matt. He settled next to Linda and placed her hand in his. The team crowded in slowly, a quiet wall of angst.

"We've stabilized him as well as we can." The young doctor's tone was strained. "But we've got to get him to a trauma center fast. I called for Med Flight. They're on their way from Little Rock."

A shadow of sorrow fell over Linda's eyes. She managed a nod and fought back the thickness in her throat.

"How bad is it, Doctor?" she asked.

"I'm not gonna lie, Nurse Stevens. His condition's critical. He took a bad blow to the head." Dr. Evans paused, his forehead creased with worry. "I'm not an expert on brain injuries. But I can tell his brain's swelling rapidly. If we don't get the pressure relieved---"

His voice trailed off. A knowing silence fell over the room. Then, Grant Edwards, a beefy lineman known for his loose mouth, asked, "Is he gonna die?"

Dr. Evans stared at the young man with heavy eyes. He was about to reply when Bobby Dalton stood to his feet.

"Take a knee, Guys," he ordered. "And link arms." He looked at Matt. "Pray, Preacher. And give it everything you've got. Don't you hold nothin' back!"

Matt grabbed Bobby's hand and knelt with the team. His words were fast and fervent. But in his heart, they felt futile. At his "Amen", the slap of helicopter blades could be heard overhead.

The sliding door leading out of the ER flew open with a loud WHOOSH! A gurney carrying Brett's tortured body emerged, pushed by three young men with tension-filled faces. Before he could stop her, a wailing Linda escaped Matt's grasp and lunged for her son. The EMT closest to her raised his arm, blocking her progress.

"Stay back, Lady! Let us do our job."

Matt's cheeks burned with anger. Before he could speak, Carol exploded.

"That's her son! Can't she see him for just a minute?"

The young man's face softened. He lowered his arm and motioned for his partners to back away. Linda crept toward Brett and took his hand in hers. She stroked it with the tips of her fingers as if willing strength into his frail form. Then she bent and, through the maze of tubes that held her son hostage, whispered, "I love you, Baby. Momma's right here."

Matt pulled her back and she collapsed into his arms. "I can't lose him, Matt," she sobbed. "He's all I've got."

"Shh," Matt whispered. "They're doing all they can."

The EMT's resumed their mission, hurriedly pushing the gurney through the throng of onlookers that had gathered outside. Carol circled Linda's waist and with Matt's help ushered her as fast as they could toward the waiting helicopter.

Halfway there, the rotor blade sliced the evening air with a sound that was half hiss and half chop. Its growing force parted the crowd nearest it, allowing the EMT's a clear path to the side door.

A Pastor's Story

Once the gurney was loaded and secured, Carol helped Linda inside. Then, she turned to Matt and pulled him to her.

"I'm going with her, Matt. I can't leave her." Her voice was shaky and strained, barely heard above the thrum of the chopper. "Get to us as quick as you can."

The two hugged tightly and then kissed quickly. Carol turned and with the help of the young man she had berated earlier, climbed inside and settled next to her best friend. Matt backed away and watched as the helicopter rose slowly against the black sky. A hundred feet up, it angled slightly to the right then bee-lined northeast into the darkness, its red and green strobe lights flashing in tandem.

For a long time, Matt stood motionless, peering upward into the moonlit darkness that had swallowed up those most precious to him. He should hurry to be with them. Instead, he remained statue-like, void of feeling. He sensed the crowd around him gradually melt away into the night until he was alone...completely alone.

And then he felt it. The same sensation he had felt that day on the bank of Miller Lake thirteen months ago. It welled inside him so fast his breath halted. When he finally caught it, he gasped with such force it drove him to his knees.

"Why, God? Why?" he pleaded.

He flung himself prostrate on the ground. But surprisingly no tears came. Only anger—burning, consuming rage that smoldered the ground beneath him. He rolled over. Above him stretched an orderly and boundless tapestry of God's handiwork. And the scene begged a question that finally did pull the tears from his eyes.

Where are you?

CHAPTER TWENTY-ONE

Saturday, September 7th, 5:10 A.M.

A chill filled the waiting room. Light from the nearby hallway spilled inside silhouetting a figure stretched out under a blanket on the couch across the way. Matt turned and glanced out the window behind him. Ghostly lights dotted the Little Rock landscape all the way toward a faint hint of dawn in the east.

His phone lay on the Gideon Bible on the table next to his chair. Powering it up, he found a host of texts and missed calls from back home. In no mood to talk, he placed it in his jean pocket.

From around the corner, a female voice laced with urgency boomed over the intercom. "Dr. Reynolds, you're needed in critical care." The name clicked inside Matt's head. "That's Brett's doctor," he said to himself, his senses suddenly alive. He sprang to his feet. Fatigue overwhelmed him, and he dropped back into the squatty chair that had turned into a make-shift bed overnight.

"Mornin, Pastuh."

For an instant, Matt thought he was imagining the greeting. Then, out of nowhere, a short, shadowy figure pushing a dust mop approached him. As he drew closer, the man's features focused in: slender build and dark-skinned with reddish-brown hair. He wore a light-colored button-down shirt with dark trousers. He looked to be mid fifty-ish or maybe even early sixty-ish. His round face sported a lazy smile behind a short, scraggly beard that matched the color of his hair.

"Rough night, huh?" the man asked, his gaze fixed on the floor.

There was something in the man's soft and pronounced drawl that put Matt at ease, and despite the urge to get to his godson, he stayed seated, somehow drawn in by this stranger. *How does he know I'm a pastor?* Matt wondered. Had they met before?

"Do we know each other?" Matt asked.

Now just feet away, the man stopped and circled his hands around the top of the mop's handle. His grin broadened and he chuckled lightly. "Maybe," he replied, shrugging. He pointed upward. "You know, we all His. So, yeah, I'd say we connected somehow."

Matt pondered the calm and cryptic reply. Then, the man spoke again, his brow arched and his tone now sober and pointed.

"You worried about yo' boy," he said knowingly and pointed upward again. "It's in the Big Man's hands now. You gotta trust Him. And you bein' a man of the Word, it's time to practice what you been preachin' all these years. To let Him work it out. That His will be done."

The words pierced Matt's heart. Who was this man? How did he know so much about what was going on? His appearance was meek and plain, but his words were powerful and packed with wisdom.

Matt stood to his feet. "Thank you, Sir" he said, extending his hand. "Thank you for your kind words."

Get to Brett!

The man grasped Matt's hand and shook it gently. There was even something special about the warmth of his touch.

"Trust Him, Broth-uh," The man cuffed Matt's shoulder and cocked his head backward. "Now, go check on yo' boy."

Matt made his way through the maze of chairs and out of the room. As he approached the double doors just around the corner that led inside CCU, he halted suddenly. What was the man's name?

In mere seconds, he stepped back through the lone entrance to the waiting room. The sleeping figure still rested under the blanket. But as quickly as mysteriously as he had appeared, the stranger had vanished.

Dr. Hiram Reynolds was a diminutive man. Thin-framed with closely cropped black hair and a thick mustache to match, he looked to be somewhere between forty and fifty. His words were direct and softly spoken. But their gravity cast a weight over the room that made Linda struggle to stay on her feet.

Matt grabbed her just before she collapsed and helped her to the chair beside Brett's bed.

Dr. Reynolds cleared his throat. "Ms. Stevens, I'm not one to mince words. Your son's brain function is down to less than twenty-five percent and it's still falling. The ventilator's breathing for him."

A crushing silence followed. Matt looked at Carol, stunned and shaking. She turned away hurriedly and burst into tears before rushing out the door.

"With brain activity that low, his quality of life would be greatly diminished," Dr. Reynolds continued. "You need to consider that in your decision."

Decision?

Matt pushed the implication of the doctor's words out of his head. He knelt beside Linda and placed his hand on Brett's exposed arm. It felt cold and lifeless, a testament to the dire news they had just been given. On the other side of the bed, the din of the ventilator echoed a harsh discord to the way life had been just hours ago.

No longer in shock and now angry, Matt shot Dr. Reynolds a sharp glare. "Why didn't you tell us last night it was this bad? We thought with time he'd be okay. And now you're telling us he's not gonna make it?"

He clutched the sides of his face and stumbled to the window. Hands fisted, he pounded them on the cold glass. "So, there's no hope?"

Dr. Reynolds' eyes darkened. He shook his head. "It would take a miracle."

Matt stepped to the foot of Brett's bed. Flashes of his godson's growing up years flooded his head and for a long minute he stood lost in nostalgia. He looked at Linda.

"She needs some time, Doctor. Time to process all this."

Dr. Reynolds nodded. "I'll check back in a little while. And I'll tell the nurses outside not to bother you."

He walked to the door and stopped to offer a heartfelt condolence. "I'm really sorry, Ms. Stevens," he said, then disappeared without waiting for a reply.

Linda remained a sitting statue, her face colorless and empty. Matt wondered if she understood what the doctor had just said. Or had her brain somehow tuned it out?

Carol entered the room, still shaky and red-eyed. Matt drew her to him and the two stood silently, overcome by the cruelty of the devastating scene before them. Through his shirt, Matt pinched his side to make sure he wasn't dreaming. A subtle pain assured him he wasn't.

Linda's body shook suddenly as if jolted awake from a stupor. She labored to her feet and gazed at the comatose body of her child. Then, she turned to face her son's godparents.

"Oh, Honey," Carol said, taking a step toward her. Linda raised her hand in a gesture of refusal. Startled, Carol halted and stepped backward.

Linda looked again at her son and then at Matt. "There's something you have to know."

CHAPTER TWENTY-TWO

Saturday, January 21, 1995, 1:00 P.M.

It was late morning when the grey clouds hanging low over Asheville let go of their icy confetti. Driven by a stiff wind with an arctic bite, the pea-sized flakes had grown to golf ball size by noon and blanketed the dead earth in a sheet of white.

Now, standing at his patio door, Matt could hear squeals of delight from children throughout the neighborhood. Across the back fence, he could barely make out the roof line of the house behind him. Another hour of this and Asheville would be a total whiteout.

He raised his cup of coffee and took a sip. Scowling, he walked to the kitchen and poured the lukewarm liquid down the drain. His fingers stroked the rim of the mug as he gazed at the cordless phone lying on the bar. It remained defiantly silent.

Carol had been gone since eight o'clock. Shreveport was a three-hour drive south, away from the snow. As much as he wished he could blame her not calling on the weather, he knew the real reason she hadn't. Her exit had been almost as icy as the scene outside. No hug, no kiss on the cheek, not even a smile. Just a cold stare and a terse "bye" before the door slammed behind her.

Matt pounded his fist on the countertop. What was up with her? Until a month ago, their five-year marriage had been like

A Pastor's Story

a honeymoon that wouldn't end. Then, overnight it seemed, something changed. She had grown distant and tight-lipped, locked in a bubble he couldn't break through. Day after day, she had tuned him out, unwilling to open up.

Late last night it had come to a head when he had lost his temper and demanded an explanation. In tears, she had retreated to their bedroom and locked the door, leaving him to spend a restless night on the couch and wonder if his marriage was on the verge of breakup.

The phone rang. He reached for it then hesitated. Its ring sounded louder than normal, even hostile in a strange way. He took a deep breath and pressed the receiver to his face. Before he could say anything, a loud sniffle drifted into his ear. He braced himself.

"Hello?"

Tense silence. Then, a woman's broken voice spilled through the phone.

"Matt?"

He recognized the voice instantly. "Linda, what's wrong?

Linda Stevens choked back a sob. "Is Carol there?"

"No, she's gone to her mother's." Matt sensed trouble. He wanted the truth. And he thought he already knew it.

"Did he hit you again?"

The sob grew to a high-pitched weep. "Yes. With his fist this time." She paused to catch her breath. "What am I gonna do, Matt?"

He wished he knew. Since first arriving at Grace Fellowship, he had prayed for his friend and parishioner Bill Stevens to be delivered from the grip of alcohol. He had counseled Bill privately, even pushed him until he signed up for local AA meetings. After the first meeting, Bill had found more than one half-hearted excuse not to go back: He didn't connect with the other attendees. The leader of the group was judgmental and self-righteous. He could quit drinking anytime he set his mind to it. Now, listening to the grief brought on by his friend's reckless folly, Matt wondered if there was any hope for Bill Stevens.

"Is he still there? Matt asked warily.

"No, he stormed out and drove off in his truck," Linda said. "He told me he didn't love me anymore."

Matt felt his face flush with anger. Bill Stevens wasn't his friend. He wasn't even a whole man. He was a coward who had chosen to ruin his life and his marriage over a mindless addiction to liquor. As his pastor, he would forgive him and keep praying for him. But no more would he allow this man—a member of his flock—to batter his own wife.

"Chain lock your doors," Matt ordered. "If he shows back up, don't let him in. I'm on my way. I'll knock four times so you'll know it's me."

He grabbed his keys and his coat and raced out the door. Meandering through the snow-covered streets to the corner of Jackson and Lee, Matt pondered what he would say when he got there. Like the God he served, he hated divorce. But he couldn't condone physical abuse.

The small brown-frame house looked painfully quiet as Matt pulled into the driveway. He switched the ignition off and sat silently for a few seconds. A prayer was in order, but the will or the words wouldn't come.

As he stepped out into the frosty air, he thought of Carol. She should be here for her best friend. Instead, she was hundreds of miles away, indulging her own selfish whims. The idea made his lip curl, and he slammed the truck door in frustration.

Matt walked to the carport door and tapped four times on the metal frame. From inside, the jingle of the chain lock could be heard.

The line, he reminded himself. *Don't forget the line.*

The house felt chilly and uninviting as Matt stepped inside. He dusted the wet snow off the arms of his jacket before taking it off and laying it on the kitchen table. Linda closed the door and secured the chain lock. When she turned around, the dim light of the room revealed a purple splotch beneath her left eye and an inch-long gash across her cheekbone. The sight made Matt's blood boil. How could a man do that to a woman?

"Oh, Linda. I'm so sorry." He wanted to reach out, to soothe the hurt and make it better. But again, he remembered the line: that imaginary border that was not to be crossed when he was alone with a female member of his flock. No physical contact. None. And ever since becoming a pastor, he had managed to follow it without fail.

Linda shrugged. "It's not the first time." She paused to reflect. "But it *is* the first time he's ever hit me with his fist. Always before it was just a hard slap."

Her eyes moistened. "It'll go away in about a week. In the meantime, make-up will cover it." She dabbed at the swollen eye. "I just wish I could make Bill's drinking go away that easy."

"Do you still love him?" Matt asked.

A shadow fell over Linda's face. "I don't know anymore. But when I think about it, I must love him, or I'd have left a long time ago."

"You don't have to put up with this, Linda."

Matt's tone was stern, like a father speaking to a daughter whose heart had been bruised by a two-timing boyfriend. "I think it's time you thought about getting out. As your pastor, I'll help you anyway

I can. Carol will too. And God will understand. He don't expect a wife to stay with an abusive husband."

She stared at the floor momentarily then walked slowly to the den. Matt followed, pondering with each measured step what else to say to her.

Through the front window, the snow was falling heavier now, a picture of serenity that stood in stark contrast to the pall that hung over the room. "Isn't that pretty," Linda said contentedly. "I can't remember the last time we had this much snow." She turned around, her tone sober now. "Is Carol's mother okay? When I talked to her yesterday, she didn't mention anything about going to see her."

Matt's reply was guarded. "Momma Ruth's been down pretty low since Pop died last August. Carol thought spending a few days with her might lift her spirits."

It wasn't all a lie. His mother-in-law *had* been depressed since becoming a widow. And Carol's going to see her *would* be good for her. Still, he felt a pang of guilt at stretching the facts.

Linda crossed her arms. "Is that really why she's gone, Matt?" she asked knowingly.

Inside his head, Matt scrambled for a comeback. Should he stick to what he had just told her? Or should he make up something else? He decided he might as well tell her the truth.

"Carol hasn't been herself for a long time. She's been really distant with me. And she won't tell me what about. Every time I try to get it out of her, she gets defensive and shuts down." He looked at Linda expectantly. "Has she said anything to you?"

Linda shook her head. "She doesn't have much to say to me lately about anything. I can tell from what little she says she's not happy." She turned again to stare out the window. "The woman doesn't realize how good she's got it. Or how lucky she is."

Linda whirled back around. "Sounds like both of us have spouses who don't appreciate us. Or what we do for 'em." She stared at Matt, brows raised. "You agree?"

Suddenly, he no longer saw a broken and bruised twenty-nine-year-old. He saw the attractive and independent woman whose face, despite its stain of abuse, now glowed with the beauty he had admired since the day he met her. And it captivated him.

His brain fogged with confusion. *Stop it! You're here to comfort and console.* He stared deep into her eyes. And what he saw was inescapable. She no longer sought his compassion. She now craved his embrace.

Without warning, Linda burst into sobs. Matt stepped toward her and extended his arms.

The line! Don't cross it!

He backed away. As her sobs intensified, she slumped forward and extended her arms toward him. "Hold me, Matt," she whimpered.

There was no second-guessing now as he stepped over the line and drew her close. She buried her face in his chest and circled him with trembling arms. As her hands caressed his back, a chill shot down his spine and he squeezed her tighter.

What are you doing? Matt's brain screamed.

You're consoling a distraught church member, he assured himself. But deep inside him, something told him this was going too far. Still, to pull away from her now would be heartless and insensitive.

"Shh!" he whispered softly in her ear as his cheek touched hers. "It's okay. You're gonna get through this. I'm here for you."

For a long minute, the two remained locked in a silent embrace. Then, Linda pulled back from him slightly and gazed up into his assenting eyes.

"You're a fine man, Matt McDonald." Her fingers brushed the underside of his chin. "I never knew just how fine 'til now."

He couldn't remember the last time Carol had spoken words like that to him. Linda was right. His wife didn't appreciate him or all he did for her. What he was feeling right now he hadn't felt at home in months, maybe years. So, when Linda pressed her lips to his, he no longer felt any urge to resist what was happening. It was wrong, he knew, but in some justifiably crazy way, it felt right.

And over eighteen years later, the fruit of this encounter would change his life forever.

CHAPTER TWENTY-THREE

Saturday, September 7, 2013, 5:35 A.M.

BRETT IS YOUR SON!

The words hung in the air with such force Matt struggled to breathe. Was it true? Was she saying the young man clinging to life in front of him was his own flesh and blood? Or was she delusional? Had the imminent loss of her child warped her mind so bad she was talking out of her head?

Matt looked at Carol. Her eyes were heavy with confusion. She walked to Linda and hugged her.

"That's right, Honey." Carol stared tenderly at Brett. "He has been like our own son ever since he was born. And no matter what happens, we'll always think of him as ours." She patted Linda softly on the back. "Why don't we sing to him like we did when he was a baby?"

Linda tore herself from Carol's embrace and stepped backward, squaring her shoulders. "That's not what I'm saying," she said firmly. Then, her tone softened. "Oh, Carol, please don't hate me. I've kept the truth from you and Matt too long."

Carol's face wrinkled. "The truth?"

"Yes, the truth." Linda closed her eyes and pressed her hands to her face. "Matt is Brett's real father!"

Carol laughed half-heartedly. "Honey, calm down. You're not making any sense." She reached out but Linda drew back again. And what she said next sucked the air out of the room.

"I have the blood test at home to prove it!"

As Matt looked on, an excruciating scene unfolded. Two women as close as blood sisters, still wearing their matching jeans and tiger tees, stood ripped apart by a short and shocking admission. The object of that admission only feet away, fighting for his life. It was cruel and unusual punishment. One had already lost her only child. Now the other was about to suffer the same fate. And in the process, they had just lost each other.

Then it hit him.

He was about to lose a second child. Probably his wife. And maybe even more!

A loud groan escaped Carol. She stared at Brett and made her way to his side. Her hand reached out and stroked his arm. Matt looked on, his heart pounding. What was next? A wail? A scream? A fit of tears? A collapse to the floor? The passing seconds were agonizing.

Just get it over with! Hit me, he pleaded silently.

Instead, she began to hum. The notes were shaky and garbled at first. Then, as they gained clarity, he recognized them: the melody to "Hush Little Baby". An image of her pushing the swing back and forth filled his head. He had blotted that scene out for months. Now, it was back to haunt him once more. As she labored through the refrain over and over, his insides roiled with anguish. Only this time around, he knew in his heart he deserved every ounce of torment he was feeling.

After humming through the song a half-dozen times, Carol raised Brett's limp hand to her lips and kissed it. Then, she lowered it back to his side and walked calmly to the chair near the door and picked up her purse.

"I'm taking your truck," she said. "I need to be alone."

With that, she was gone.

Matt felt a tug toward the door. He should follow her. Instead, he walked to the side of the bed and reached out to caress Brett's thick brown hair. "My son," he whispered low.

As he studied Brett's face, Matt wondered why he had never noticed what he saw now. The curvature in his son's upturned nose mimicked his own. The two of them shared high cheekbones and the same angular chin. And for the first time, Matt noted Brett's attached earlobes—a fairly rare trait he had been told was highly genetic.

"Are you not going after her?" Linda asked, rushing to his side.

"No." Matt replied, his tone deadpan. He walked to the window and stared out at day's first light. "She needs time to herself. Besides, what would I say to her right now?"

Linda bent and kissed Brett on the cheek. "I wanted to tell you and Carol the truth years ago, Matt. I really did. But I knew what it would do to the two of you. To me and Carol. And your ministry at the church. I just couldn't bring myself to do it."

She settled into the chair by the bed. "I couldn't put it off any longer. You had to know so you can give your son a proper goodbye."

Matt walked to the foot of Brett's bed. "You found out through a blood test? How, Linda? And when?"

She stared at the floor. "I felt so guilty about it. But the opportunity was there, and I just couldn't pass it up. Before that day, I made up my mind that I'd live without ever knowing for sure."

"What day?" Matt asked.

"That Sunday in August of '98. It was the summer before Brett turned three. Our church held a back-to-school blood drive." She sighed heavily and looked up at him. "You donated."

Matt's mind raced backward to the events of that day. And a detail he had wondered about at the time but didn't' question suddenly made sense. After the bag was full, the woman who drew his blood had drawn six vials instead of the usual three.

"The woman who drew my blood, instead of filling three vials, she filled six. Did she know what it was for?"

Linda grinned. "That was Becky. She and I were in nursing school together at U of A. I didn't know she was working the drive that day. When I walked in the fellowship hall and saw her, I sensed an opportunity knowing you had signed up to be a donor. I asked her if she would draw the extra vials from you like it was normal. And I would explain later."

"So, what happened after that?" Matt asked, suddenly intrigued by her plot.

"When she slipped them to me as they were packing up to leave, I told her to call me later, when we could talk. I went home and put the vials on ice. When she called me that night, I told her what was going on and asked her if she knew of anybody I could take them to for analysis. She told me about a friend of hers who worked as a lab technician at the DNA testing center here in Little Rock. I think Becky had helped this woman out a lot when they worked together in Hot Springs. She called in a favor."

Tears moistened Linda's eyes. "I still had to get a sample from Brett." She reached over and caressed his cheek as a tear rolled down each of her own. "I don't remember why, but I had a syringe in the medicine cabinet at my house."

Grief shook her body. "He was just two. I had to hold him down to stick the needle in his arm. He didn't understand why his mommy was hurting him so bad. I think I cried harder than he did."

She walked to Matt and buried her head against his chest. "I'm so sorry, Matt. I wish now I'd have left well enough alone and gone on without knowing. I've ruined your marriage. I've lost my best friend. And now we're gonna lose our son."

Matt circled her with his arms. A sense of déjà vu washed over him as memories of a snowy morning in January long ago overwhelmed him. Then an image of Bill Stevens holding his newborn son flashed in his head. Bill had turned over a new leaf in the wake of Brett's birth. But the novelty of fatherhood had faded a short year later. And the lure of alcohol had pulled him back to his old ways and eventually brought about his demise. He had gone to his grave not knowing the truth.

"Have you thought much through the years about that morning?" Matt asked. "How it happened?"

Linda freed herself from his embrace and walked to Brett's bedside. "I was hurting physically. You were hurting emotionally. We let our pain turn into passion. And there was no turning back."

His cell phone buzzed inside his pocket. It was Bobby Dalton. Matt pressed the phone to his ear. "Hey, Bobby."

"How's he doing, Preacher?" Bobby asked, his voice muffled by a mechanical rumble.

"Not good, Coach," Matt replied soberly. "He's on a ventilator. We're being told there's brain damage."

There was burning silence except for the hum of what Matt suddenly recognized as the drone of a school bus engine.

"The team's with me," Bobby said. "We're about a half hour out. I'll call you when we get there. It may take me a few minutes to find a place to park the bus."

"Drive safe, Coach," Matt said.

He tapped the red circle on his phone and looked at Linda. "Bobby and the team'll be here shortly. I need to go down and prepare 'em."

Matt exited the room and made his way down the corridor to the elevator. As he stepped inside and pressed the lobby button, Carol's distraught face flashed inside his head. "God, protect her," he prayed aloud. He had to get to her, to plead his case, and try to win her forgiveness.

But when? Right now, he couldn't leave his dying son.

CHAPTER TWENTY-FOUR

Saturday Morning, 6:28 A.M.

The lobby was heavy with the smell of strong disinfectant that burned Matt's eyes. He washed his face at the water fountain then dried it with the handkerchief in his back pocket.

Glancing down the short hallway to his right, he spotted a wall directory. Left arrows pointed to the cafeteria, gift shop and administrative offices. But it was the arrow pointing the other way and the word "chapel" beside it that caught his eye.

As the door closed behind him, he breathed in a stuffiness that told him the room was seldom entered. Except for a lighted mural on the front wall, of Jesus holding a lamb in his arms and surrounded by a flock of sheep, a pale darkness filled the room. He walked slowly up the narrow center aisle and settled into the padded pew to his right.

Amid the stale air around him, he felt a reverence as he gazed at the image of the Good Shepherd. He managed a smile and thought of Grandma Effie, his grandmother on his momma's side. Saintly to her core, she had displayed an 8 X 10 version of the same scene on the wrinkled wallpaper in her bedroom. To everyone else it had been just a picture. But to her it had been a treasure, faded and yellowed, a timeless reminder of where her hope had rested.

He dropped to his knees and clasped his hands together. His plea was simple.

"God, forgive me."

There was no verbal reply. Not that he expected one. Nor was there a still small voice. Only the sound of mundane voices outside the door he had just entered. He bowed prostrate and pressed his hands to the cold floor.

He thought of King David. Chosen and blessed by Almighty God. And in a moment of weakness framed by unbridled lust, he had lost favor with the same God Who had anointed him to lead His people. The price paid being the loss of his own child.

"Please don't take my son!" he cried out.

In a flash, he was back in the hostile waters of Miller Lake, flailing wildly, gasping for breath, surging to the surface, begging a silent and indifferent God not to take his child. Then he was on the bank, crying uncontrollably as he pounded his fists into the hard ground, anger pouring out of him in waves. God hadn't heard his plea. Instead, He had allowed a paltry feathered creature to lure his child to her death. Even now, as he again pounded his fists to the floor in frustration, he couldn't' fathom it.

But he knew the hard truth. That day standing at the water's edge, as divers had pulled Angel's lifeless body from that murky dungeon, he knew then it was punishment. Sin was not without consequence. He had preached that to his congregation over and over. And, just like David, it had turned out to be his own undoing. As he had held Angel's limp form in his arms, rocking her back and forth, he knew his adulterous tryst had cost his child her life. Now, that same, selfish act was about to claim the life of his son—the young man it had produced.

"Yo' boy's gonna live."

Matt bolted upright. Was he hearing things? His eyes panned the room. In front of him, Jesus remained quiet, his eyes still on the lamb He cradled in His arms.

I've heard that voice before, Matt thought.

He stood to his feet. Now he was sure he wasn't hearing things. He turned and stared toward the back of the room. His eyes now tuned to the shadowy darkness, he was able to make out the silhouette of a human form standing between the two back pews. He recognized the figure instantly. It was the same man he had talked with earlier in the waiting room.

The mop he had held earlier was gone. Now, a flimsy, white cloth dangled from his hands. He ran it gently over the top of the pew in front of him as he made his way toward the center aisle. He walked forward, a broad grin lighting his face.

"He's gonna make it, Pastuh," the man said in a hushed tone. "Yo' prayer's been answered."

Matt studied the man closely. What was it about him? His appearance was unassuming, but somehow it gave off an energy that was mystical. And, curiously, how did he know so much about what was unfolding with Brett?

"Who are you?" Matt asked.

Ignoring the question, the man moved behind the front pew to his left and lightly ran the cloth over its wooden back. He stopped suddenly, stared intently at the mural, and began to sing.

There is a name I love to hear

I love to sing its worth.

It sounds like music in my ear

The sweetest name on earth!

Matt looked on, bewildered, as the man continued his task, moving the length of the pew toward the wall while occasionally eyeing the image of the Good Shepherd. His scratchy tenor voice rose and fell with the quiet shuffling of his feet.

Oh, how I love Jeee-sus!

Oh, how I love Jeee-sus!

Oh, how I love Jeee-sus!

Because he first loved me.

The man retraced his steps and stopped a few feet short of the pew's end. He looked straight at Matt and sang the last line again, drawing out each word with a fervor that sent a vibration throughout the room.

"You 'bout to get the good news," the man said, his eyes shining.

A hair-raising second later, Matt felt his cell phone shudder inside his jean pocket. He pulled it out. The name staring up at him sent his heart racing. He placed the phone to his ear as Linda's frenzied words confirmed what he already knew.

"He's awake, Matt! He's awake! Get up here now!"

A lump tightened his throat. "I'll be right there."

The man inched close enough to gently pat Matt's shoulder. He winked, then turned and ambled slowly down the aisle, humming the tune to the hymn he had sung moments before, the same hymn Grandma Effie had taught her "Matthew Boy" at the age of four.

Matt turned and stared tenderly at the face of Jesus. "Thank you, Lord," he whispered.

When he turned back, he wasn't surprised at what he didn't find. Just like he had earlier, the mystery man had disappeared.

CHAPTER TWENTY-FIVE

Saturday Morning, 7:10 A.M.

Bending over his young patient, Dr. Reynolds traced the stethoscope up, down, and across, listening intently. Underneath it, Brett's exposed chest rose and fell in a heaving motion. Matt studied Dr. Reynold's face. Was it disbelief? Or a look of wonder that the doctor's own words had been borne out right before his own eyes? That the unexplained had just happened.

Dr. Reynolds stood upright. He looked at Brett and shook his head. Then he turned his gaze to Linda and Matt as a smile broke across his face.

"I can't explain it. His heart rate and blood pressure are back to normal rhythm. His pulse is strong. His temperature is near normal." He paused and looked again at his patient. "Something miraculous has happened here."

Linda buried her face against Matt's chest and sobbed. He draped his arm around her shoulders and leaned down to whisper in her ear, "Our son's okay."

Immediately, Carol's face flashed inside his head. Guilt snagged his heart and held on with a force that pulled his arm free. He walked toward the door, wishing, begging silently for a solution to this war of allegiance waging inside him. But nothing rushed to his defense.

Brett moaned suddenly. A loud cough propelled his body forward. In a flash, Dr. Reynolds placed his hand on Brett's back and eased him back onto the pillow.

"Take it easy, Son," he said, patting Brett's shoulder. "Try not to raise up, okay? Stay as still as possible. Doctor's orders."

"What happened?" Brett asked through a labored gasp. "Where am I?"

Dr. Reynolds backed away as Matt and Linda moved closer. Linda bent and kissed her son lightly on the lips. "You got hurt during the game last night. Your helmet came off and another player's helmet hit you in the head."

"Is he all right?" Brett asked, his voice filled with concern.

"He's fine," Linda replied. "Get some sleep, okay? We'll talk later. I'll be right here when you wake up. And so will Uncle---" Matt and Linda's eyes locked. "Uncle Matt's here, too."

"I'm thirsty," Brett pleaded as his hand explored the bandage circling his head. "Can I have some water?"

Linda grabbed the plastic pitcher on the table by the bed. She leaned in and guided the straw to Brett's lips. He swigged three strong gulps.

"Don't give him too much," Dr. Reynolds ordered. "His swallowing might be slow to come back. We don't want him to get strangled."

Matt was about to speak when his cell phone buzzed inside his pocket. "Hey, Coach."

"What's it lookin' like, Preacher?" Bobby asked, his tone guarded.

"You're not gonna believe it, Coach. He's awake. And everything looks to be back to normal."

Bobby let out a loud yelp. "He's awake, Guys! He's gonna be okay!"

Raucous hollering pounded Matt's eardrum and he backed the phone away. He walked outside and leaned against the wall, waiting for the noise to die down.

"What happened, Preacher?" Bobby asked. "I mean, what turned it around. Do we know?"

"His doctor says there's no medical explanation." Matt paused, overcome with joy. "It's a miracle, Coach."

There was a long silence as both men processed the gravity of the words. Abruptly, the door opened, and Dr. Reynolds stepped outside.

"Hold on a minute," Matt said, then lowered the phone to his side. "What now, Doctor?"

"I've ordered a CT scan to make sure we're not missing something. Somebody from radiology will be up in about an hour to get him." He smiled broadly and cuffed Matt on the shoulder. "He's a fine young man. And given what's happened, I'd say God has plans for him. Big plans."

As he watched Dr. Reynolds walk away, Matt felt an assurance of what he'd always suspected. That Brett was destined for something great. The doctor's words had just confirmed it.

He raised the phone to his ear. "You still, there, Coach?"

"I'm here. Listen, Preacher. None of these guys got any sleep last night. And they ain't eat anything since noon yesterday. I'm gonna take 'em to the cafeteria and vouch for 'em, then I'll be there. What floor and room number?"

"Fifth floor, critical care. Get off the elevator and turn left. Follow the signs. He's in room nine."

"Got it," Bobby said. "See you in a few."

Matt pressed the red circle and dropped the phone in his pocket. He felt faint all of a sudden. It was like the word cafeteria had unleashed the hunger pains he had managed to suppress for hours now. And he knew someone else had to be famished, too. He pushed open the door and eased inside.

"He's drifted off," Linda whispered. "Hopefully he'll sleep 'til they come to get him for the scan."

Looking at Linda confirmed his hunch. She appeared gaunt, unsteady on her feet almost. "Linda, you need to eat something. What can I go get you?"

She thought for moment. "A package of sandwich crackers and a power drink. And a snickers bar, jumbo size. That should tide me over for now."

"I saw a couple of vending machines around the corner. I'll be back."

He turned to go but stopped when he felt a tug on his arm. "Matt, you have to get home to Carol. You can't wait any longer."

He nodded in agreement. Then he remembered. He was on foot.

The scan revealed an all clear. In Dr. Reynolds' words, it was like there had "never been a head injury to start with." Still, he strongly recommended that Brett remain in the critical care unit for at least one more day for close observation, a decision Matt and Linda both agreed was for the best. In the meantime, the revelation of Brett's paternity would remain untold to him. That, they agreed, was also for the best.

After Brett was wheeled back from radiology, it took a full ten minutes to coax Dr. Reynolds into allowing the team to visit him.

And even then, only five at a time were allowed into the room. With thirty-five players at ten-minute intervals, the clock on the wall ticked by ever so slowly. Finally, at 11:30, the last quintet of Tigers sauntered through the door. As they gathered around Brett's bed, Linda motioned Matt outside.

"How long do you think we should wait before we tell him?" Linda asked.

Matt pondered briefly. "Not too long. And we need to tell him together."

She stared at the wall with heavy eyes. "Do you think we need to tell him before he leaves the hospital?"

"Maybe," Matt said. His train of thought redirected. "I don't know what'll happen when I get home, Linda. I've got a feeling it won't be good." He shrugged. "Who knows when I'll be able to get back up here."

Linda's eyes moistened. "Matt, I'm so sorry about all this. I feel like I've ruined your life. And Carol's" She dropped her head. "She'll probably never speak to me again."

"As uncertain as everything is for all of us right now, I can't help but be happy in a way," he said, managing a grin. "I have a son." His tone grew worrisome. "I just hope he'll accept me as his father."

The room door creaked open, and Bobby Dalton walked out followed by five beefy Tigers still wearing orange and black jerseys. Coach slapped Matt hard on the back, then drew Linda in for a loose hug.

"That young man's incredible!" he said. "I've never met a finer young man, Ms. Linda. His daddy would be so proud of him if he were here."

If you only knew, Matt thought.

"Yes, Bill would be proud," Linda said, shooting Matt a sheepish glance that told him she hated faking the truth. "Very proud."

Bobby turned to his players. "Go on down, Guys. Round everybody up. I've gotta get you boys back to Asheville."

"I need a ride," Matt announced. "Carol had to leave earlier and took my truck."

Bobby frowned. "I wondered where she was. Everything all right? As crazy as Carol's always been about that boy, I figured wild horses couldn't have drug her away from him."

Matt's brain scrambled for an explanation. His head was blank. "She's okay," he said. Then, before Bobby could reply, he turned hurriedly toward the door. "I've gotta tell him bye. Go on down. I'll be there in a few minutes."

He closed the door behind him and drew in a long breath. Across the room, Brett lay motionless, obviously asleep. He made his way to the bed and stared down into his son's face. Again, he wondered how he had been blind all these years to the facial similarities the two of them shared. It didn't matter. All that mattered now were the years they would share going forward.

As father and son.

Sandwiched between the hum of the motor in front of him and the loud and incessant chatter of thirty-five spirited teens behind him, it was impossible for Matt to focus on the trip home. He needed to concentrate, to come up with a dialogue in pleading his case. But the rough-riding bus coupled with all the noise around him crowded out any chance of it.

As the bus passed the city limit sign, Matt rose from his front-seat perch and stepped to Bobby's side. "Can you drop me off first?"

he asked, struggling to mask the anxiety that by now had his stomach in knots.

"Sure, Preacher," Bobby replied cheerfully. His face grew stern. "You sure you're okay?"

"I'm just tired," Matt replied. "My nerves are still frayed from what happened. I just need to get home."

Bobby nodded and Matt settled back into his seat. Two traffic lights and four stop signs later, the bus lurched to a stop alongside 810 West Oak Street. Bobby shifted into park, pulled the door open, and turned around in his seat. "You're home, Preacher. Go crash for the rest of the day."

Considering what he knew was about to happen, Matt found the words eerily prophetic. By now, the chatter behind him had quelled somewhat. He really should say a few words of encouragement to the team. But as his mind wrestled with what waited for him inside, he was short on words. Reluctantly, he stood to his feet.

"Hang in there, Guys," he said. "We'll get him back as soon as we can." He smiled and forced a fisted hand into the air. "Go Tigers."

"Thanks, Brother Matt," the team chorused.

"I'll keep you posted, Coach," Matt said as he stepped outside.

The door hissed and closed behind him. As the bus pulled away, Matt walked slowly up the driveway to the carport. He leaned against the back of his truck briefly before moving on to the door leading inside to enemy territory. "It's in your hands, Father," he whispered aloud.

He closed his eyes, turned the knob, and pushed the door open.

CHAPTER TWENTY-SIX

Saturday Afternoon, 3:50 P.M.

It was back.

That chilly air of combat that had ruled his home after Angel's death hung in the kitchen. Three months ago, it had seemingly vanished overnight. Now it had returned with an almost caustic feel, wrapping around him with frigid tentacles.

Matt shook off its grip and crept quietly to the den. The house was totally quiet except for the tick of the hall clock. He checked the back patio. It was still and lonely. He walked to the door that led to the living room. It appeared as always. Wasted space, never disturbed. That left one other path to take. The long walk down the hall to the bedroom.

She stood at the window, facing away from him, staring outside. Still dressed in orange and black, her arms were folded across her upper body, her shoulders slumped. Even from across the room, Matt noticed a shine to her cheek where dried tears had washed away the makeup that had been there earlier. The sight made his heart ache, and that anguish surged inside him when she reached up and brushed away fresh moisture beneath her eye.

He walked to the bed and sat down. The mattress creaked loudly. She turned her head slightly then quickly resumed her mute gaze out the window. He knew it would be this way. She was a master at the silent treatment. And after a long and painful year of it following Angel's death, it still cut to his core.

He stared at the floor. "Brett's gonna be fine."

He let the words hang in the air. Would they stir something inside her? After all, Brett had been like her own child since birth. Would the good news melt away that frosty façade?

Seconds ticked by, then a full minute. More icy silence.

"The doctor couldn't explain it. He said the only explanation was a miracle."

Still nothing. He rose and walked to her side. "We need to talk."

Her lips pressed into a firm line. She breathed deeply then turned to face him.

It was a déjà vu moment. A replay of the night he had brought up taking the swing down. When the two of them had faced off in a battle of stares. Only this time, the anger that poured from her eyes seemed more venomous than then. As he pondered what to say, all he could muster was a weak "I'm sorry."

The words had barely left his lips when it happened. Carol's hands had always been vessels of warmth, immune to any motion not tender and caring. So, when her outstretched palm landed squarely across his left cheek in a hard slap, Matt struggled to process his wife's sudden aggression. He lowered his head and clutched his jaw as a stinging pain stretched all the way from his chin to his earlobe.

"I'm listening," she said smugly.

Dazed and still in disbelief at what had just occurred, he retraced his steps to the bed and sat down. As the pain slowly faded away, he gathered his thoughts.

It was time to tell a story.

"That day's haunted me for over eighteen years now. Looking back, I still can't believe it happened." He paused to massage his still-tender cheek. "Remember the big snow?" he asked rhetorically. "It was January of '95. A Saturday morning. You went to your mother's. All mornin', I worried about you drivin' that far on slick roads."

Out of the corner of his eye, he saw Carol turn back to gaze out the window. Hoping for a reply of some kind, he hesitated.

Nothing.

"When the phone finally rang that morning, I figured it was you calling to tell me you'd made it there safe." His tone grew somber. "But it was Linda. Calling for you. She was crying and so upset. Bill had grabbed the bottle early that morning. He got drunk and hit her with his fist. Then he stormed out. She was terrified he'd come back even drunker than when he left."

He paused to let the drama sink in. Carol sniffed loudly and wiped her face. Was she feeling guilty that she hadn't been there for her best friend? Was she feeling Linda's pain? Were his words softening her?

He pressed on.

"I drove over there to be with her. She was in tears and her eye was swollen and purple," Matt said, choking back anguish as the image of her bruised face replayed inside his head. "I reminded myself on the way there to keep my distance. Like I always did when I counseled a woman from the church." He shook his head, guilt now crushing in around him. "But I didn't."

"She was beside herself. Distraught. I hugged her and—." He stood to his feet and walked back to his wife's side. "Carol, you have to believe me. I never meant for it to happen. Linda didn't either. And I swear to you, I didn't know 'til this morning that Brett was my son."

Carol remained stoic and statue-like. Deflated, Matt turned away, his shame suddenly so raw his knees shook, forcing him back onto the bed. He hung his head and waited, for what he wasn't sure. The passing seconds were agonizing, physically painful almost. As he kept his eyes glued to the floor, he thought his heart would explode.

"Get out!"

Having pronounced sentence, she marched past him and out of the room. Immediately, the hall clock clanged at quarter hour, a sound that seemed to signal a death knell for twenty-four plus years with the woman he loved. Inside him, emotions raged. Part of him felt relief that it was over. The rest of him screamed, *Don't give up! Fight on!*

He pulled his large two-wheeled suitcase from under the bed and hurriedly stuffed as many clothes as he could into it, leaving a vacant corner for his travel-sized toiletry case. Pulling it behind him, he stepped into the hallway. On the wall in front of him, in two rows of four each, hung an octet of 8X10 portraits that chronicled the growth of a dollish infant all the way up to a pixie-faced and precocious eight-year-old.

He studied the pictures closely. Each one offered up its own memories, all echoes of happier days. He pressed his finger to the glass of the last picture taken of his daughter and traced the outline of her smile.

"I love you, Angel," he whispered.

When he reached the door that led out to the carport, Matt turned and looked around at the safe haven that had been home for so long. Just feet away, Carol stood at the glass door that led to the patio, again facing away from him in defiance.

"I'd appreciate it if you wouldn't talk to anybody about this before tomorrow morning." He pulled the door open. "I'm resigning the church."

As he stepped outside, reality struck like a punch in the gut. In a matter of hours, his days as pastor of Grace Fellowship would be over.

End of Part Three

CHAPTER TWENTY-SEVEN

Saturday Afternoon, 5:10 P.M.

Matt clutched the bronze, praying hands bookends to his chest and closed his eyes. He could still feel the warmth of Grandma Effie's touch from thirty years ago as she had placed them in his hands and covered them with her palms. "They're yours now," she had said smiling. "Make me proud. Just think, my Matthew Boy might be the next Billy Graham."

What would she say to him if she were here now? Would she be disappointed in him? Chastise him for his misdeed? Or would she substitute a grandmother's steadfast love, instead?

Pushing the likely answer out of his head, he gently placed the bookends on top of the other keepsakes packed loosely in the plastic tub on his desk. He looked around him. The credenza sat empty except for a thin layer of dust. Squares of mismatched paint marked spots where his seminary certificate, Sallman's Head of Christ, and images of biblical figures had hung on the wall for over twenty years. All that was left to pack lay hidden inside his desk.

He dialed Jerry's number. After three rings, his head deacon's gravelly voice boomed forth.

"Hey, Preacher! I just heard the good news about an hour ago."

Matt mustered what little exuberance he could. "Yeah, he's gonna be okay." His voice turned solemn. "Jerry, I'm here at the church. I've gotta talk to you."

Silence filtered through the phone. "Right now, Matt?" Jerry asked, his tone now subdued. "I'm a mess from workin' on my truck. Could we do it tomorrow mornin' before church?"

"No, it can't wait. I need you to come now."

After a brief hush, a loud breath spilled from the phone. "I'm on my way."

Matt motioned to the chairs in front of his desk. "Sit down, Brother."

Jerry sat down and nodded toward the tub. "Is this some kinda joke, Preacher?"

"No joke," Matt mouthed, his voice barely audible. "I wouldn't do that to you, Brother."

Jerry leaned forward and stared down. When he looked up, his eyes were clouded with sadness. "So, this means what I think it means? You're leaving? Why, Matt? What brought this on?"

While waiting for Jerry to arrive, Matt had wondered how he would break the news. Now, he could think of only one way to do it. One word. One name.

"Brett."

Frowning, Jerry leaned back slowly. "What about Brett? He's gonna be okay, ain't he? What does he have to do with this?"

In an instant the anguish Matt had been holding inside boiled over into raw frustration at his own immorality. "He's my son!" he blurted out.

Jerry pushed back fresh sweat from his temples. Confusion etched itself in the lines across his forehead. "You've always claimed him like he was yours. Ever since Bill died, you and Carol have been like second parents to him. I don't see---"

"I'm his **real** father, Jerry," Matt interrupted. "His biological father. And I think you can figure out real quick what that means."

Jerry stared at his pastor. The color that had briefly returned to his cheeks drained away again, faster than it had earlier. "You and Linda?" He swallowed hard. "Had an affair?"

For Matt it was crushing, crippling almost, to hear his name and Linda's paired in the context of adulterous behavior. How many lives would this revelation change? How much hurt would his selfish act inflict?

"It wasn't like that, Jerry," Matt replied. "We both got caught up in a weak moment. Carol had gone to her mother's. Bill got drunk and hit Linda then left in a rage. I went over to comfort her. We embraced and it went too far."

Jerry eyes narrowed with skepticism. "You're telling me this was a spur of the moment thing? And that it only happened one time?"

"I'm telling you the truth, Jerry," Matt said, his hand raised as if swearing an oath. "And yes, it was just one time." He lowered his hand. "Jerry, I didn't know until this morning that Brett was mine. When we thought we were gonna lose him, that's when Linda told us."

"Us?"

Matt's body slumped. "Me and Carol."

Silence fell over the room. Neither man spoke for a long and dark moment. Finally, Jerry rose and walked to the window. "How's she handling this news?"

"Not good. She's at home. It's like she's in a daze. I tried to talk to her right before I came here. She wouldn't listen to me. Told me to get out."

Jerry turned around. "So, what are you gonna do now, Matt?"

Matt didn't hear him. He had a question of his own. "Will you promise me something?"

Jerry walked back to the chair. His hands gripped the top of it. "I'll do what I can depending on what it is."

Matt stared at the tub. "Let Carol stay in the parsonage. At least for a while. Until I can try to make things right with her." He looked up. "I don't know if I can, but I want to try to win her back."

Jerry sat back down. "I'll go by and check on her when I leave here, Matt. I'm sure she needs some time to sort all this out." He shook his head from side to side. "I never dreamed you'd leave us like this, Pastor" he said, choking back emotion. "I'm gonna miss you."

At mention of the word pastor, Matt thought about tomorrow morning's service. "Jerry, I have to get back to the hospital early in the morning. I know that puts you in a bind for tomorrow. But Linda and I have to tell Brett the truth together before he finds out another way."

Jerry nodded. "I'll talk to the other deacons tonight. We'll figure something out."

Matt reached forward and joined hands with his head deacon. "I am so sorry about all this, Jerry. I've failed you and so many others." He strengthened his grip. "You've been a true friend, Brother. I hope we can still be friends in spite of all this."

Jerry wiped a tear away. "A twenty-year-old friendship don't just go away," he said. "Now you promise me something."

"I'll try," Matt said.

"Promise me you won't let this ruin the rest of your life. You're still young, Matt. You've got good years left. Find a new way to serve God."

Jerry's words sounded useless and unreachable. *How was further ministry even possible?* A fall from grace most likely meant shunning, possibly outright rejection, by even those he considered his closest friends. Still, Matt couldn't tell his friend no.

"I promise," he said firmly.

Jerry eyes narrowed. "Where you goin' for the night? You're welcome to stay with me and Helen. I'm sure she'd understand."

"I'm headed to Chuck's when I leave here," Matt replied. "Since all this happened, I hadn't even checked on him."

Jerry squeezed Matt's hand so hard a pain shot up the underside of his arm. "Easy, Deke," Matt said, wresting his hand free and managing a smile. In return, Jerry winked and grinned broadly.

Matt's heart warmed. It felt good knowing at least this friendship would go on.

"How is he, Linda?" Matt asked.

"He's doing okay," she replied. "He's wondering why Carol's not here. I told him she had been and that she was so exhausted she had to get some rest." Her tone grew guarded. "I think he suspects something's not right."

"I'll be there early tomorrow morning. We'll tell him then."

"How did it go with Carol?" Linda asked.

"Not good. She told me to get out," Matt said. "I packed my things and left. I'm on my way to Chuck's for the night."

"Oh, Matt," Linda said, her voice wavering. "I'm so sorry. You don't deserve this."

"I just cleaned out my office. I left Jerry crying in the parking lot."

Linda's sobs drifted into his ear. "Matt, how do you think Brett's gonna react tomorrow when we tell him? After what his body's been through, I'm afraid he might relapse somehow."

"He has to know the truth, Linda," Matt said firmly. "We can't put it off."

"I know," Linda agreed. "I'm just scared."

"Don't be. He's strong. He'll be shocked at first, but he'll handle it in his own way. Trust me, he will."

As he finished speaking, the cone-shaped roof of Chuck's house focused in above the tree line bordering Baker Creek. "I'm at Chuck's, Linda. I'll see you early tomorrow. Get some sleep, okay?"

"I'll try."

He pulled off the highway and onto the worn path that led down to Chuck's house. As he approached the house, Matt felt a strange vibe, like the house itself was sending a message, one he wasn't sure he wanted to understand. He parked, got out, and walked slowly to the ramshackle porch. As he made his way up the steps, an odd sensation sent a quiver through him.

He pulled open the unlatched screen door and stepped inside. Chuck lay on his back on the couch, his head nestled against his left shoulder. A peace colored his face, accented by a curvature of his lips that produced a slight grin. His hands lay folded across his waist, clutching a white envelope.

Matt walked to the couch and knelt. He reached out and took Chuck's right hand in his own. It was mortally cold. For a long and sorrowful minute, he stroked its lifeless flesh. As he did so, a burning truth struck him. In barely twelve short hours, one life dear to him had been spared while another one had been taken.

The words of Job echoed inside his head: "The Lord giveth and the Lord taketh away."

CHAPTER TWENTY-EIGHT

Saturday Evening, 8:15 P.M.

Matt watched as the hearse bounced down the path, its black bulk barely visible in the fallen darkness. It circled wide and lurched to a stop about ten feet from the porch. The door flew open, and Wendell Maddox stepped out.

"Hey, Preacher," he said. "You just find him?"

A short dumpy man with a cue ball head, the town's lone mortician sported his usual maroon necktie and white short-sleeved shirt splotched and ringed with sweat. Known far and near for his drab get-up, he was even more notorious for his coarse mannerism that contrasted starkly with the genteel expectation of his job.

"About fifteen minutes ago," Matt replied. Though annoyed by Wendell's curt greeting, he had expected nothing less, having witnessed the same lack of empathy many times in the past.

"Good man," Wendell said, wiping away a ridge of perspiration from his forehead. "Chuck was a little different. But in a good way. He'd help anybody. Never wanted for much of anything." He walked to the back of the hearse and looked around briefly before opening the back door and pulling out a folded gurney. "You can tell that by the looks of this place."

"Let me help you with that," Matt said. He grabbed one end of the gurney, and the two of them carried it inside and set it down at the end of the couch. As Matt watched, Wendell raised the gurney to its highest level, then turned and grabbed Chuck's hand. Finding the envelope tucked under it, he pulled it out, gave it a quick glance, and handed it to Matt. Scrawled across it in shaky handwriting were the words Pastor Matt.

"I'd say that belongs to you." As he continued holding Chuck's hand, Wendell's face pinched with study. "From how stiff he is, I'd say he's been dead since early this morning."

The undertaker's crude words irked Matt. "Let me help you get him in the car," he said, struggling to hide his irritation.

When the gurney was secured inside the hearse and the back door closed, Wendell turned and gripped Matt's shoulder. "I'm really sorry, Matt. I know you two were close." He extended a sweaty hand, and the two men shook firmly.

"By the way, Chuck came to see me about a month ago," Wendell said, his tone less abrasive. "He wanted to go ahead and pay me for when this happened. He said to give his ashes to you to spread in the creek back there. I'll let you know when they're ready to be picked up," he said before climbing in and driving away.

As the dim taillights faded into the darkness, all of the day's angst suddenly welled inside Matt'schest. He wanted to scream but was too tired to. He stared up into the starlit night.

What now, God?

The door creaked loudly as he closed it behind him and secured the chain lock. The envelope stared up at him from the oak table by the front door. He tore it open and pulled out its contents: a piece of lined, yellow paper and two keys. Across the top of one key, a small shred of paper with the word *"house"* had been taped. The other key he recognized as one to a bank safety deposit box. He laid the keys on the worn cushion next to him and unfolded the letter:

Hey Pastor,

I hope your the one that found me. It's Saturday mornin about five as I'm writin this down. My time's short. Real short. And dependin on how quick I go, maybe I won't lay here too long before you or somebody comes. Awhile back, I talked to Wendell at the funeral home and paid him to cremate me. I told him to give you my ashes to sprinkle in the creek out back. But if you don't want to bother with it, don't. Cause I'm with my love, Louise and Baby Charles now.

The house is yours. Do what you want to with it. Go see Miss Margaret down at the bank. She'll let you in my lock box. Everything thats in there's yours. So's the little dab of money I've got in my account. Spend it on whatever you want to.

Pastor, I want you to know you're the best friend I ever had. And a darn good preacher, too. I hope I never done anything to hurt your feelins. If I did, just know I didn't mean to. And I'm sorry.

You had it rough when you lost your little girl. And when Carol blamed you for it. But you got through it. Now keep tellin folks about the Lord. That's what its all about.

I'll give Angel a hug for ya.

Chuck

He tucked the letter back in the envelope and dropped the keys in his pocket. As he looked around the room, a reality settled over him. This was his home for now.

A Pastor's Story

Carol's face flashed inside his head. Jerry would have checked on her by now. A part of him wanted to know how he had found her. The other part told him it could wait until morning.

He turned off the drop bulb that hung suspended over the couch. Darkness flooded the room. Feeling his way to the bedroom, he searched the wall near the door for a switch but didn't' find one. By the moonlight that filtered in through the open window, he felt his way across the room to the bed and pulled back what felt like a cotton blanket. He removed his shirt and shoes and reclined backward. Beneath him, the bed was hard and unyielding. And the air in the room felt warm and sticky. It would be a restless night.

And tomorrow...what would it bring? How would his son react to the truth? Would Jerry be the bearer of bad news? Was his marriage over? He shuddered and closed his eyes.

Outside, down the hill by Baker Creek, a band of bullfrogs croaked in flawless symphony. The refrain floated freely through the open window, soothing his ear and temporarily crowding out his worries. It was the same sound that had enriched his childhood on many a summer night as he lay in bed. And now, once again, he found himself captivated by how such small and petty creatures could command the night. For hours he listened. Until finally, exhaustion intervened. It was after 1:30 when he finally fell asleep.

CHAPTER TWENTY-NINE

Sunday, September 8th, 6:25 A.M.

Predawn shadows were fast disappearing as Matt pulled onto the highway and headed into town. As expected, it had been a fitful night. His back ached from a mattress that felt like it had been filled with corn shucks and a few cabbage heads thrown in. His legs cramped from all-night bending in a bed a foot too short. And his temples throbbed from forty-eight hours of life-altering emotion. But the physical ache paled in comparison to the anxiety coursing through his whole body. In a few short hours Brett would know the truth.

How would he react?

The possibilities clouded Matt's head as he braked to a stop at the light at Perkins and Main. As he waited, his thoughts shifted to Carol. What state had Jerry found her in when he had checked on her last night? Angry? Distraught? Disgusted? Afraid?

He had to know.

He glanced at his watch: 6:31. Being an early riser, Jerry was up by now, probably still in a haze over yesterday's revelation. Suddenly, the vehicle behind him blasted its horn. Glancing up, he saw the light had turned green. He veered left, leaving the rude driver in his wake, and grabbed his phone lying in the seat next to him. Tapping Jerry's number in, he waited.

"Mornin', Matt." Jerry's voice lacked its usual joviality. "How was your night?"

"Not good," Matt replied heavily. "I don't know if you've heard yet, but Chuck's gone. I found him when I got to his house last night."

Jerry breathed loudly into the phone. "Good ole Chuck. A finer man never walked the earth. Had he been dead long?"

"Wendell estimated he probably died early yesterday morning," Matt said. "He'll be cremated. No funeral."

"You on your way to the hospital now?" Jerry asked.

"Headin' outta town right now. Did you go by and check on Carol last night?"

"I did."

A silence filled the phone, like Jerry didn't want to continue. Matt's heart raced. When Jerry finally spoke again, it raced even faster.

"I'm worried about her, Matt. Really worried. She seems worse now than after Angela died."

Matt's chest tightened. "What exactly did she say?"

"That's why I'm worried. She hardly said anything. Just stared into space most of the time." Then, a revelation that grabbed Matt's breath. "She finally told me she felt like she didn't have anything to live for."

The words rattled Matt's brain so hard the phone slipped from his hand into his lap and down to the floor mat. In his scramble to get it back, the truck swerved onto the shoulder of the highway. He jerked the steering wheel to the left just before the right front tire contacted the shoulder's edge. Shaken, he braked to a stop.

"I'm turnin' around, Jerry. I've gotta talk to her. I'd never forgive myself if she did something drastic."

"Matt, you can't," Jerry said timidly. "She left town early this mornin'."

"Did she say where she was going?" Matt asked, panic rising in his voice.

"No. She said she needed some time to herself. She gave me an envelope to give to you. It feels like there's just paper in it. I didn't ask any questions. Just told her I'd give it to you when I saw you."

Matt paused for a long and calculating minute. "I don't know how long I'll be at the hospital. Depends on how Brett's doing and how he takes the news." He took a deep breath. "I've gotta know what that paper says."

"I'll take it by the parsonage and leave it on the bar," Jerry said. "I know you've got a lot on your mind. Drive safe."

"I'll be back as soon as I can," Matt replied, then dumped the phone in the seat beside him.

He pulled back onto the highway, his mind a blur. Soon, Brett would learn the truth. A truth that would change his son's life and his own forever. Right now, though, he couldn't help but wonder if another numbing truth was about to play out. That he might never see the love of his life again.

On the back side of the hospital parking lot, Matt squeezed his F-150 between a grey sedan and a white Chevy blazer. He cut the engine and unwrapped the breakfast sandwich he had picked up at a drive-thru eatery minutes earlier. As famished as he was, the biscuit looked less than appetizing. When he bit into it, he discovered why. Its rubbery texture almost made him heave, but he found the will to wolf it all down. The coffee in the console next to him turned out to be equally bland, lukewarm and bitter. Still hungry, he told himself the vending machine in the lobby might be his next stop.

He scrolled through his contacts and found Linda's number. After five rings, she answered.

"Sorry. I didn't want to answer it in the room. I'm right outside the door. Are you here?" she asked.

"I'm in the parking lot. Gettin' ready to head up. How's he doin'?"

"He's good. Itching to get out of this place. Dr. Reynolds was by about thirty minutes ago. Checked him out one last time. Then, he left to start the discharge procedure."

"Wow," Matt replied. "What a difference a day makes."

"One of the nurses has a son about Brett's size. She ran home and got him some athletic shorts and a tee shirt. She found him some flip flops, too. They're a little small, but they'll get him out to your truck and then on home."

"I hadn't even thought about you two bein' stranded here," Matt said. "But my brain's been everywhere since Friday night."

"Matt, have you talked to Carol anymore? I'm worried sick about her."

He stepped out of his truck and leaned against the side of it. "She left town early this morning. I talked to Jerry on the way up here. She gave him an envelope with a note inside to give to me."

"She didn't give him any idea where she was going?"

"No. She just said she needed time away to sort things out. Be prayin' she don't do anything desperate."

"You know I will. She's like my sister." Her voice cracked. "I just hope she doesn't hate me over all this."

Matt closed the door to his truck. "Did you tell Brett I was coming?"

"No. Matt, I want to get Brett home before we tell him. I've got to get out of this place. And the sooner the better."

"I agree," Matt said. "I'm headed up."

He hurried across the parking lot and raced up the concrete steps leading to the hospital entrance. As he neared the glass vestibule, he noticed the back of a masculine figure kneeling in the shrub bed to his right. The man wore a white mesh baseball cap, a light blue shirt, and dark trousers and held a small pair of pruning shears in his hand. With measured precision, he snipped at the uneven sprigs of a large boxwood that tickled the brick façade of the building.

Drawing even with the man, Matt froze. There was something about him that seemed familiar. Then, he recognized him. It was the mystery man from Friday morning.

Matt watched as he stood upright and laid the shears on top of the boxwood. He turned and flashed Matt the same warm smile he had when their paths had crossed in the waiting room and the chapel. Shaking his head, the man chuckled lightly.

"Well, looks who's here!" His tone resonated with glee. "Mornin', Pastuh!"

Again in awe of the man's engaging demeanor, Matt reciprocated an uneasy grin. Something told him not to speak, to wait for what he was sure would be simple but sage advice. Would it be words he wanted to hear?

"So, you here to take yo' boy home, I s'pose." He paused and stared heavenward then back at Matt. "God's good, ain't He?"

Matt didn't answer. He sensed there was more to come. And while a part of him craved to hear it, the rest of him cringed with dread at what it might foretell.

"He'll need a little time. When he finds out the truth, I mean. But he's a fine young'un. Smart, too." The man smiled again, bigger than before. "You and him'll be fine," he said, kneeling to resume his task.

Relieved, Matt walked slowly along the sidewalk, digesting what he had just been told. He had taken only a few steps when a quiet voice inside him told him the man had more to say. He turned around just as the man stopped trimming and looked his way.

"Don't give up on her, Pastuh," he said with a wink. "She still loves you."

Hope welled inside Matt. He raised his hands and pressed them against his chest in a gesture of unspoken prayer. "Thank you," he mouthed silently.

"Goodbye, Pastuh," the man replied with a tone of finality. "And good luck."

Appearing satisfied that the once ragged bundle of leaves was now a perfect sphere of green, the man made his way out of the bed and down the sidewalk, eventually disappearing around the corner of the building.

Something told Matt he would never see the mystery man again. And the thought saddened him.

CHAPTER THIRTY

Sunday Morning, 9:10 A.M.

As he walked toward Brett's room, Matt scarfed down the last cheese cracker from the package he had just bought in the lobby and chased it with a swig of Diet Coke. He thought of the mystery man again, halfway expecting him to appear out of nowhere. But the only person in sight was a young lady in scrubs behind the counter at the nurse's station. She looked up and smiled as he walked by then quickly fixed her gaze back on the computer screen in front of her.

Arriving at room nine, he pressed the side of his face to the door and heard conversation between two male voices. He waited for a break in the dialogue, then pushed the door open and walked in.

"Good morning, Folks." He walked to the foot of the bed and tossed the empty soda can and the cracker wrapper in the trash. "Doc, I hear we're ready to get this young man outta here."

Dr. Reynolds stood bedside, holding a clipboard. "You're the preacher, right?"

"That's right. I'm his pastor," Matt replied while convincing himself it was as much the truth as it was a lie.

Dr. Reynolds stared at his young patient. His face was a mix of awe and disbelief. He hugged his clipboard to his chest and shook his head.

A Pastor's Story

"Young Man, in my twenty-five years as a neurosurgeon, I've seen a lot. But I've never witnessed anything like this. Less than two days ago, I was sure I was gonna lose you. And now, except for that," he said, pointing to the bandage just behind Brett's temple, "I wouldn't know anything ever happened to you."

Brett sat on the side of the bed wearing a blue, number nine Dallas Cowboy's jersey, white nylon shorts, and black flip flops. Linda sat next to him, her arm circling his waist, her face beaming. She leaned over and kissed him on the cheek.

"We're so blessed!" she exclaimed. "It's a miracle."

Dr. Reynolds grinned. "I can't argue that." He looked at Matt. "Evidently the Man Upstairs is not through with this young man."

"Are you a Christian, Doctor?" Matt asked.

"I am. I couldn't do what I do if I wasn't."

"Then you know that God's still in the business of changing lives. And He can do anything He wants to do."

The door pushed open and a short, thin elderly woman with silver hair and thick-rimmed glasses entered pushing a wheelchair. She looked at Brett. "You ready?"

He raised his hand in refusal. "With all due respect, Ma'am, I'd like to walk out of here on my own two feet."

The woman looked at Dr. Reynolds for support. He cocked his head and shot her a look that told her she had made the trip for nothing.

"Let's grant this young man his wish, Miss Davis. He deserves it after what he's been through."

Perturbed, the woman pivoted and huffed out of the room, striking the door with the handrim of the wheelchair.

'Hope her day gets better soon," Matt said.

"She's one of our auxiliary volunteers," Dr Reynolds said. "You'd think they own the place."

"I'm sure glad I called her 'Ma'am'," Brett said.

The four burst into raucous laughter.

"I can't believe Aunt Carol didn't ride up with you. Is she okay?"

Matt merged onto the interstate. He had wondered how long it would be before Brett asked about her. In the rearview mirror his eyes locked with Linda's.

"She took some medication yesterday to help her sleep. It caused some kind of reaction. She was still in bed when I left this morning."

A preacher shouldn't lie. That truth cut deep.

He looked in the rearview again. Linda's expression told him she felt his pain and sympathized with his words. But it didn't lessen the shame he felt at lying to his son.

"So, who preached in your place this morning?"

Matt hadn't expected this one. "Jerry said he'd get one of our lay ministers to fill in."

A preacher shouldn't lie twice. That truth cut even deeper.

Change the subject!

"You hungry?" he asked. "You hadn't had much chance to eat the last two days."

Brett rubbed his stomach. "I ate a big breakfast. Eggs, bacon, pancakes, fruit, and juice. It wouldn't all that bad. Kinda goes against what I've always heard about hospital food."

"Bet it wasn't as good as Mom's cookin', was it?" Linda asked.

"Not even close," Brett laughed. "Think you might whip us up some biscuits and gravy tomorrow morning?"

"I'll bet I can," she replied cheerfully.

Brett looked at Matt expectantly. "Can we run by the field house on the way in so I can get my truck? The keys are in my locker and so is my phone. If you call Coach, I bet he'll meet us there."

Before Matt could answer, Linda interjected. "I'll drive you to school tomorrow morning. I hate to bother Bobby on a Sunday afternoon."

Brett sighed. "Okay. I've done without 'em both for two days. One more won't kill me."

Two hours and four more bothersome fibs later, Matt pulled his truck into the driveway at 1010 South Jackson Street. He stared at the faded, brown siding of the modest home. And suddenly, visions of a snowy morning eighteen and a half years earlier swirled inside his head. Even now, what had played out that morning behind those walls still dazed him. That it had actually happened. That he had *let* it happen.

"Home sweet home!" Linda exclaimed as the three crawled out of the truck. "This place never looked better."

Inside the house, Matt and Linda sat quietly at the dining table, waiting for Brett. When he emerged from his bedroom, he wore a pair of his own loose-fitting athletic shorts and a tank top and carried the castoff garments in his hand. "Let's give these to Goodwill," he said, tossing them on the bar. "They're not in bad shape. Some kid can use them."

The air tensed suddenly. Matt felt butterflies in his stomach. He and Linda hadn't talked about how to bring the subject up. Or which one of them would reveal the truth.

"Did you call and check on Aunt Carol?" Brett asked.

"No. She's probably still asleep," Matt said.

Linda stood to her feet. "Sweetie, Matt and I need to talk to you."

The color drained from Brett's cheeks. "What's wrong? Is it Aunt Carol? Has something happened to her?"

Matt stood and draped his arms around his son's shoulders. "No. Nothing's happened to your Aunt Carol." He motioned toward the living room "Let's all sit down."

As the three of them settled onto the couch, Matt looked at Linda. "Your mom has something to tell you, Brett."

CHAPTER THIRTY-ONE

Sunday Afternoon, 1:15 P.M.

As he placed his hand on Brett's bare knee and squeezed it tenderly, the feel of his own flesh and blood sent a tingle through Matt's palm. He looked at Linda. She appeared frozen in thought.

Finally, as she stroked the top of her son's hand, she spoke.

"Sweetie, yesterday morning before you woke up, Dr. Reynolds told us he didn't think you were gonna make it. I thought I was gonna lose you. I was in shock."

Matt braced himself, thinking her next words would spill the truth. To his surprise, she digressed.

"Bill was a good man." She pushed back her hair and gazed toward the picture window. Her tone was heavy now with sentiment. "When you were born, I saw a soft side of him, a side I had never seen before. He wanted so much to be a good father to you." She looked back at her son and wiped away a shameful tear. "And for the short time he had with you, he really tried."

Matt heard the delay in her voice. *Don't prolong this,* he pleaded silently. Then, calmly and matter-of-factly, she delivered the partial truth.

"Bill was not your real father, Brett."

Stiff silence.

A Pastor's Story

Matt studied his son's eyes. Was it shock he was seeing? Or disbelief framed by confusion? When Brett finally spoke, his response drew a gasp from his mother.

"So......are you trying to tell me I'm adopted? That you're not my real mom?"

Linda leaned in and rested her head on her son's shoulder as more tears came. "No Sweetie, that's not what I'm saying. I gave birth to you. You're the best thing that ever happened to me."

Brett pulled away from her slightly. "Then who is my real dad, Mom?" His voice grew shaky. "Is it anybody I know?"

Feeling like his heart would explode inside his chest, Matt released his knee grip and clutched his son's hand. **"I'm your real father, Brett."**

Linda clenched her eyes shut and wiped the tears from her cheeks. "Sweetie, I swear I was gonna tell you next month when you turned eighteen. Please don't hate me!"

Brett stared at Matt. "You're my dad?"

No words would come. All Matt could do was nod. He watched as Linda turned away, fearful of whatever would happen next. A thickness filled the room, so heavy Matt found it hard to breathe. He stood and walked to the window, gathering both thought and breath along the way. Outside, across Jackson Street, two spirited youngsters frolicked and squealed beneath a drooping mimosa tree. *That's how life's meant to be*, he told himself. Happy and simple. And he found it amazing, stunning even, that only a stone's throw removed from that peaceful and fun scene, a long-held secret now revealed had turned a young man's life upside down.

Brett stood to his feet. He shook his head as if trying to rid his brain of what he had just heard. He walked across the room, then turned around to stare at his mother. His tone was hostile now. "So, you had an affair? You cheated on your husband with your pastor. Your best friend's husband? That's what happened, Mom?"

Linda shook her head. "It wasn't an affair." She looked at Matt then back at Brett. "We got caught up in a weak moment. And one thing led to another. It just happened."

"How does something like that just happen, Mom?" Brett asked. A quiet and sarcastic chuckle escaped him. "Neither one of you stopped to think about how it might hurt the ones you love?" He looked hard at Matt. "Does Aunt Carol know?"

"Yes, since yesterday morning. When your mom told both of us the truth at the hospital."

Brett frowned with confusion. "Wait! Are you saying you didn't know either?" He looked back at his mother. "You kept this from everybody 'til two days ago?"

Linda buried her face in her hands. "Yes!" she wailed. Sobs shook her body. "Yes, I've lived with it for all these years. I didn't want to ruin Matt and Carol's marriage. I didn't' want to destroy his ministry. But when I thought you were gonna die, I felt like I didn't have any choice but to tell the truth. Then, he could tell you goodbye as your father, not as your pastor." She stared pleadingly into Brett's eyes. "You can understand that, can't you, Sweetie?"

Brett looked back at Matt. "This is why Aunt Carol hadn't been at the hospital. Why she didn't ride up with you this morning. She's gotta be devastated."

Matt choked back a surge of anguish as he nodded. "She left town this morning. I don't know where she went. She left a note with Jerry. It's on the bar at the parsonage."

Brett exhaled loudly. "So, he knows, too. Does everybody in town know about this by now?"

Matt's anguish faded, replaced by a wave of boldness. "Son, hear me out." He paused briefly, wondering how to begin. "Your mom's husband was a good man in a lot of ways. But he had a demon—alcohol. One that turned him into a bad man when he was under its power. That Saturday morning, he got drunk and hit your mom in the face. Then he left here in a rage."

An image of Linda's swollen and purplish eye filled his head. "She called the parsonage to talk to Carol, but she'd left town early that morning to go see her mother in Shreveport."

"Your Aunt Carol and I were having problems of our own then," Matt said reflectively. "I was worried that morning we were headed for a separation. I was gonna stay home all day, think about what I could do to try to save our marriage. But, when I found out why your mom was calling, I knew she didn't need to be by herself. So, I drove over here."

He stared out the window again. "She was distraught when I got here. At her lowest point I hugged her. And from there...." His shoulders slumped with guilt. "What happened after that is still a blur, even now."

Matt gazed back at his son and waited for a response. For an extended minute, no one in the room spoke or moved, all three motionless and stoic in a silent standoff. Then, Brett reached up and plucked the bandage from his temple. He squeezed it angrily in his palm and hurled it to the floor before turning and walking out of the room. Seconds later, his bedroom door slammed, hard enough that Matt felt the wooden floor beneath his feet tremble.

He'll need some time.

The words of the mystery man raced through his head. *How much time?* Matt wondered.

You and him'll be okay.

I want us to be more than okay, he told himself. *I want to be a father to him!*

"We have to give him some time," Matt said. "He's overwhelmed by all this right now." He walked to Linda and hugged her. "Let me take you to get your car."

Ignoring him, she pulled free and hurried down the hall to Brett's door. "I'm going with Matt to get my car, Sweetie. I'll be right back." She tarried briefly for an answer, though not expecting one. "I love you, Sweetie."

Inside the truck, Matt remained speechless as Linda cried all the way to the stadium. As he pulled alongside her vehicle, he was suddenly hesitant to leave her. "Are you sure you can drive yourself home?"

"I'll be okay," she assured him, wiping her eyes on the sleeve of her blouse. "I think I'll just sit in my car for a while and try to gather my wits."

He reached over and patted her hand. "This is all gonna be okay. You'll see. He'll be fine. Just don't push him."

"I'll try not to," she said weakly. "I just hope he doesn't stay holed up in his room long. That'll drive me crazy."

He thought of the note. "Linda, I've gotta get to the parsonage and find out what that note says."

"Please let me know" she said. "I feel so terrible about all this."

"I will," he nodded. "And don't blame yourself."

She climbed out of the truck and into her SUV. As Matt backed away, guilt at leaving her in such a fragile state flooded over him. But that guilt quickly faded at the thought of an envelope lying mutely in a house only blocks away. For he knew that what that envelope held inside it would likely shape his future forever.

CHAPTER THIRTY-TWO

Sunday Afternoon, 2:25 P.M.

Matt tore open the envelope and pulled out a page of pink stationery. He unfolded it and began reading:

> *Matt,*
>
> *I don't know how long I'll be gone. It's gonna take me some time to sort all this out. My emotions are all over the place. One minute I'm telling myself it's all a dream and that it will pass when I wake up. But then I realize I'm not asleep and that it's real. That's when I feel bitter. Bitter that you broke our marriage vows and you kept it from me all these years. But then I start to feel guilty that maybe it's my fault. That I wasn't a good enough wife to you. That I didn't measure up like a preacher's wife should. And maybe that's why you turned to Linda for comfort. I just can't make sense of it. And what's even sadder is that I had just found the peace to move on from losing Angel. And now my world is turned upside down all over again. Don't worry about me. I'll be okay for now. I'm taking my phone but PLEASE don't call or text me. I'm not taking my debit card. I have*

enough money to last me for a while. I just need time to think. To figure out what my future might look like. And if you'll be a part of it.

Carol

Matt pressed the paper to his chest. *If you'll be a part of it.* He could almost feel the words bleed off the paper and seep into his heart. Since Friday morning, when the truth had come out, the fear of losing her had been real. But to see that possibility written down, by her own hand, cut him to the quick.

"Don't give up on us, Sweetness," he whispered.

As he folded the letter and placed it in his shirt pocket, he thought of the stash. Since June, a small envelope tucked between the mattress and box spring of the master bed had held the thousand-plus dollars left over from the church's love offering. Something told him it was not there anymore.

Curious, he walked to the bedroom and lifted the corner of the mattress. Sure enough, the envelope was flat, empty of the twenties and smaller bills it had once held. In his head, he tried to calculate how long a thousand dollars and change might last her. Weeks? Months? However long, if it ran out and she hadn't returned, what would she do then?

He walked back up the hall and collapsed into his recliner. This room: it had once been a sanctuary, a warm and safe harbor where countless games of Go Fish and Old Maid had been played, where untold hours of Blue's Clues and Sponge Bob Square Pants had been watched, and where hours of light and humorous family talk had made life in the McDonald house a fun place to be. Now the same room felt cold and clammy, void of the love and warmth it once held.

For a full half hour, amid the quiet and the chill, Matt sat completely still, immersed in memories of happier times. Then, the doorbell rang.

Brett stood against the front of his father's truck, his arms resting on the hood. Matt stepped outside and slowly closed the door behind him.

"Hey," he said.

His son stared straight ahead. "Did Aunt Carol say where she went and how long she'd be gone?" Matt walked to the side of the truck and leaned against it. "No, she didn't. I have no idea where she is or when she'll be back." He paused before adding, "She asked me not to call or text her."

Brett shifted in place. "She's overwhelmed by all this. I can just imagine how confused she's feeling. Because of me, everybody's world is messed up right now." He laughed lightly. "If I'd never been born, all this wouldn't be happening. I feel like that man from the *Wonderful Life* movie."

"Son, don't blame yourself for any of this. You've brought nothing but joy to all of us all your life. I know your Aunt Carol feels the same way."

Brett looked away. A tear trickled down his cheek and came to rest on his upper lip. Then, out of nowhere, he delivered a bombshell. "Mom just told me she has cancer. Found out last Thursday when she went for her yearly checkup." He reached up and dabbed the tear away. "It's ovarian, stage four. And it's spread to her lymph nodes."

Matt's brain fogged as the reality hit him. Linda could be dying.

For the first time Brett looked his father squarely in the eye. "She insisted I come over here and tell you I accept you as my dad. All my life you've been my pastor. And now I find out you're my real father." He closed his eyes and swallowed hard. "And on top of that, I find out I may lose Mom. That's a lot to take in at one time."

"Did your mom say when she'll start treatments?" Matt asked, still dazed by the news.

"She told me she's not gonna take any," Brett said. "Her doctor told her it might buy her a little time. But it would be torture on her body."

The two stood motionless for a long and painful minute, both at a loss for words as they absorbed what no treatment meant. Then, Brett walked calmly to the back of the truck as if he were leaving, stopped suddenly, and turned around.

"I'm gonna tell Coach Bobby tomorrow I'm quitting football. I wanna spend every minute I can with Mom," he said. "You, me, Mom and Aunt Carol. The four of us have always been a family. And we're family now more than ever. Mom needs her best friend to help her get through this. You said Aunt Carol asked you not to call her. But that doesn't mean I can't."

Matt nodded in agreement. "You're right. She'd want to know. And the two of them need to make things right. The quicker the better."

"As soon as I can get to my phone tomorrow mornin' I'm gonna call her," Brett replied. A smile curled his lips. "I love you, Dad."

"I love you too, Son."

Darkness had just fallen as Matt pulled up to Chuck's house. He switched the engine off and reclined back against the head rest. Brett's 'I love you, Dad' rolled through his head time and again, cuddling him inside. But as heartwarming as those words made him feel, he ached for his son and what the days ahead would hold for him. For a long time, he sat unmoving, staring through the windshield into the murky night, telling himself over and over what he had so often preached to his flock. That all things work together for the good of those that love Him. And for the first time ever, he found it hard to convince himself of that truth.

It was hunger that finally drove him indoors. Inside the kitchen cabinets, the only thing he could find even close to appealing was a can of Spam and a half-full sleeve of ritz crackers. He checked the refrigerator and found a jug of orange juice. It was an odd medley of sustenance, but it somehow managed to satisfy his cravings.

Preoccupied, he retreated to the back porch. The evening air felt crisp from an early-September cool front that had swept through last night. Down by the creek's edge, the band of bullfrogs had once again begun their nightly refrain. And as he stood against the wood railing of the creaky structure, reliving the events of the past two days, he couldn't help but ask himself a simple but probing question.

What now?

CHAPTER THIRTY-THREE

Monday, September 9th, 9:15 A.M.

It was musty inside the vault at Asheville Community Bank. As he watched Margaret Newman struggle to fit the guard key into its slot, Matt's mind mulled what might be hiding inside Chuck's safe deposit box. Antique coins? Old newspaper clippings? Arrowheads he had unearthed on the banks of Baker Creek?

Sensing her frustration, he thought of offering his help. But, like everyone else in town, he knew her reputation. Now in her thirty-ninth year as the bank's Senior Operations officer, the tall and slender octogenarian, with sagging cheeks and auburn hair fashioned into a tight French twist, was all business and fiercely independent. So, he waited.

After a taxing minute, she finally managed to insert the key and rotate it counterclockwise a quarter turn. "I hate these older boxes," she said, her gravelly voice heavy with annoyance. "When they're not opened for years, they get cantankerous. I bet Mr. Wilkins hadn't been in this one since Reagan was in office."

He found her words callous. Still, he shoved her coldness aside. He was here to empty the box and get out as soon as he could. Brett should have talked to Carol by now. And what his son had found out was what weighed inside his head.

A Pastor's Story

"Your key should fit the other opening." She pointed to a free-standing metal table just feet away, against the wall to her left. "If you want to, you can use that, or there's an alcove down the hall." With that, she brushed past him and out the vault door, closing it behind her. "Bring the empty box to my office when you're finished. I'll need to make sure you got everything out of it," she added before walking away.

After pulling the box out of its cubicle, he placed it on the table. Inside lay a short stack of papers, topped by a land deed from Chuck to Matt file-marked January of 1997, bearing out proof of what Chuck's farewell letter had revealed. Under the deed was a faded, black and white picture of a twentyish looking Chuck, standing next to a young woman wearing a flowered, knee-length dress and holding an infant. His wife Louise and Baby Charles. In contrast to Chuck's modest and often unkempt appearance since Matt had known him, his friend was clean cut and dapper, dressed in what looked to be a white suit with a checkered bow tie and dark, dressy shoes. He flipped the picture over. Scrawled in pencil were the words *Easter Sunday, 1965. Charles, 4 months old.*

At the bottom of the stack lay a bulky, white, legal-size envelope with a return address that read: *The Pentagon, Washington, D.C.* A quick glance inside revealed honorable discharge papers from the U.S. Army.

Nothing eccentric. Just three items that summed up a life and told a story, one of simplicity, selflessness and sorrow. Why life had dealt his dear friend such a bad hand, he would never understand. He stuffed the deed and the picture into the military envelope and exited the vault.

As he laid the empty box on her desk, Ms. Newman offered her first warm words. "I'm sorry for your loss, Mr. McDonald. Mr.

Wilkins was a good man. A simple man, as frugal a one as I've ever known." She raised the box at an angle and peered into the covered section at the back, then lowered it back to the top of her desk. A smile creased her lips. "From what I know, he thought very highly of you."

"Chuck was the best friend I've ever had," Matt said wistfully. "I'm gonna miss him. A lot."

Satisfied the box was void of all contents, she placed it on the return to her right, then retrieved a letter-sized sheet of paper from the opposite corner of her desk. "Did you know you were also the beneficiary of the funds in Mr. Wilkins' checking account?"

Matt nodded. "He left me a note telling me I was to receive what was in the box and in his account. Being the simple guy he was, he dealt mostly in cash. There's probably not much in it."

She grinned smugly. "While you were in the vault, I printed off a current statement of his account. I'll need a death certificate to close it out. If you'd like, we can transfer it to your own account with us. Or we can issue you a certified check."

With that, she placed the statement on the desk in front of him. Highlighted in yellow at the bottom of the page was the balance, a figure that made his eyes widen.

$154,688.32.

Matt switched the ignition off. A *little dab of money*. What would he do with that much? He didn't' get the chance to ponder long. In the seat next to him, his phone vibrated.

"Hey, Brett."

"Hi, Dad." An anxious silence followed. "I talked to Aunt Carol a few minutes ago."

Matt's chest tightened. "How did she sound?"

"At first really down. But the more we talked, she sounded better, more upbeat."

"Did she say where she was?"

"No. And I didn't' ask her."

"Did she say when she might be back?"

"I told her about Mom and asked her if she'd come back for her," Brett said. "She said she'd be back by the end of the week."

Matt felt a rush of relief at the news. His excitement was tempered, however, by what Brett said next.

"She asked if she could move in with me and Mom."

"What did you tell her?"

"I told her she could. Thought it might help heal what's happened between her and Mom."

Matt couldn't put the question off any longer. "Son, did she say or ask anything about me?"

"No. But I did tell her what I told you yesterday. That we've always been a family and we're still one. And we all need to come together for Mom's sake."

"Did she agree?"

"She just said she'd do all she could to help Mom." His voice weakened as he added, "And me."

The words shook Matt inside. "I've gotta go, Son," he said, opening his truck door. "Let's talk later."

"Bye, Dad."

Matt slammed the door shut. Amid the calm of the crisp fall air around him, he stood deflated as the truth sank in. In Carol's mind, Linda was innocent. All the blame rested with him. And now, somehow, he would have to find a way to win her back.

His heart told him it wouldn't be easy.

CHAPTER THIRTY-FOUR

Monday Morning, 11:30 A.M.

As he walked up the sidewalk at 321 Magnolia Street, images of his first trip here over twenty years ago flooded his brain. The tan clapboard siding had eroded to a dull white. The once-shingled roof had been replaced by a ruby red, metal one that bounced the late-morning sun into his eyes. But it was the crepe myrtle at the stoop's edge that stood out the most. Barely waist high back then, it now towered above the porch, its orchid blooms nestled lazily along the roof's edge.

He approached the door with both guilt and dread. Guilt that he hadn't already called her. And dread at how this visit would go. As he raised his hand to knock, her voice beckoned him inside.

"Come in."

Trilby sat in a wingback chair in the far corner of the small living room. She wore a navy robe accented with pink flowers. Her hair was unbrushed and her face bare of makeup. As he closed the door behind him, she raised the small turquoise teacup she held to her lips and took a slow sip. Grapefruit juice, he told himself. She swore by it.

"Have a seat," she said, motioning to the sofa under the picture window.

"I'm sorry I didn't call sooner," Matt said as he sat down. "I'm sure you know about all that's happened since Friday night." He lowered his head. "And that I resigned the church."

She set the cup on the small table next to her chair. "Jerry filled me in when I got to church yesterday. I knew something was up when I passed your office and glanced through the glass and saw your walls bare. He happened up about that time and pulled me aside. Told me everything."

Matt leaned forward. He started to speak but stopped when she flashed her palm in a gesture of silence and, in her motherly tone said, "Let me tell you a story, Son."

Matt leaned back, his mind racing. Trilby pushed back her hair, placed her hands in her lap, and calmly announced, "I knew the truth about Brett years ago."

Matt's jaw dropped. How could she know? As his brain struggled for the answer, she continued, her voice heavy with reminiscence.

"When Billy and Linda first moved here, they visited around at several churches in town. After a couple of months, they decided to make Grace their church home." She took another sip of juice, then lowered the cup to her lap. "Billy came with her for a while, but it didn't take long for him to lose interest. Even then, his drinking was a problem. And it was starting to show up on her. If you know what I mean."

She paused. When she continued, her tone was mixed with sadness and regret. "I felt so sorry for her back then. She wanted to be a good wife to Billy. I think she felt like it was her duty to change him. But he didn't want to be changed. And from what Linda told me, his daddy had the same problem. And his mother fought a losing battle with him, too."

Matt watched as a tear trickled down Trilby's cheek. She wiped it away and set the cup back on the table.

"For some reason, and I still don't know why, she took a likin' to me. I think it was because the church ladies her age at that time were reluctant to let her in any of their cliques. She'd come by about once a week, either after she got off work or early before she went in, to drink a cup of coffee with me. She did most of the talking. I was happy to listen."

Trilby looked at Matt and smiled. "Then, you were called as our pastor. And Carol and Linda hit it off right away. I was so happy to see her have somebody her age she could bond with."

The smile faded and her eyes darkened. "It was cold that Monday morning. Right after a foot of snow the Saturday before. Some of it was still on the ground. I had got to the church early and had just sat down at my desk when Linda walked in my office. You had called to tell me you were gonna be late." She winced. "That turned out to be a good thing."

It was coming in to focus now for Matt. *Monday after a big snow on Saturday.* There had been only one snow event of that magnitude during his time here. The day he had gone to Linda's house when Carol was out of town.

"She was distressed. In a state of grief almost. I first thought it was from the beating she'd taken from Billy. She tried to cover it up with eyeshadow, but the dark part of the bruise bled through it. But that wasn't what was bothering her. She told me she had been unfaithful to Billy and couldn't decide if she should tell him or not. Obviously, given his violent temper, she was afraid of what he might do to her."

Another pause. This one longer and more tense.

A Pastor's Story

"She didn't tell me who the man was. And I didn't ask. I consoled her as best I could and prayed with her about whether she should come clean with Billy. She never told me if she did. I'd be willing to bet he went to his grave not knowing."

A question burned inside Matt, one he could no longer hold in. "So, when did she tell you it was me?"

"She didn't," Trilby replied matter-of-factly.

Matt frowned with confusion. "Then how did you know?"

She shifted and sighed deeply. "Four years ago, at our spring potluck after Sunday morning service, I was sitting across from Linda and Brett." Her gaze shifted briefly to the window, then back at him. "You know, when she got pregnant, I did the math and figured out real quick that the other man was just as likely the boy's father as Billy was. And that day, as I studied Brett's face, I started to wonder if maybe I wasn't looking at a young version of you."

"I brushed the idea off for a few minutes." She paused reflectively. "And then he laughed. And it was like something inside me knew, without any doubt, that he was your son. It was the way he laughed and his body language. It was undeniable."

"Did you ever tell Linda?" Matt asked.

"No. I decided then and there that I'd leave well enough alone. 'Til that day last June."

Matt's eyes narrowed. "So, you did tell her?"

"No. I'm talking about the talk you and I had in your office that morning after your twenty-year celebration service. Or what was supposed to be one." She tilted her head, brows raised. "You don't remember what I told you that day?"

The scene came rushing back. And he remembered the one thing she had said to him that day that had left him shaken, like it did even now.

204

Don't keep anything from Carol.

"I wish you'd told me that day that you knew. I don't know if it would have made any difference. But I understand why you didn't."

Trilby clutched her robe close. "Jerry told me Carol left town. Any idea where she went?"

He shook his head no. "Brett called her early this morning. She didn't say where she was, and he didn't ask. He did ask her if she'd get back as fast as she could. Now that we know how sick Linda is."

Trilby looked bewildered. "What are you talking about?"

"Linda has cancer," Matt replied, the words catching in his throat. "Stage four ovarian. She may not have long."

A pall fell over the room as Trilby digested the dire news. "That poor woman," she said, shaking her head sadly. "She's been through so much. It's just not fair."

"I know," Matt agreed. "I just hope she and Carol can reconcile after all this. Even if there's no forgiveness for me, I hope the two of them can make things right."

Trilby stood and walked to the couch. She sat down and took his hand in hers. "You've asked God to forgive you, haven't you?"

"Yes," Matt whispered. "Many times."

"Then I'm sure He has. But something tells me you haven't forgiven yourself."

"It's hard, Trilby. I've caused so much heartache to the ones I love. I've let down the congregation I've pastored for over twenty years now. How do I forgive myself for all that?"

She squeezed his hand hard. "I'm not sure. But if you don't, you'll never find a way to minister again. And if that happens, you'll let both yourself and God down."

How he would miss this woman who had become like a mother to him! Her wit, her wisdom, but most of all her friendship.

Suddenly overcome with shame and out of words, he rose to leave. "I need to go."

Before he could escape, she stood up and pulled him to her in a tight embrace. He could feel her tiny frame trembling. "I love you, Matt," she managed to utter through a swell of sobs.

"I love you too, Trilby," he replied, fighting back tears of his own as he scooted out the door.

Once inside his truck, he sat drained by the encounter. Making those around him sad seemed to be the norm in his life right now. It was a sobering reality. And he hated it!

As he turned the key in the ignition, his phone pinged with a text from Brett. The words on the screen made his heart flutter.

Aunt Carol's here.

CHAPTER THIRTY-FIVE

Monday Afternoon, 1:30 P.M.

The left rear bumper of the van still wore the dent from that frigid night in January almost two years ago. On her way home from a women's Sunday School party, black ice and below-freezing temperatures had colluded to send the van spinning, then plummeting rear first down a steep embankment just outside town. Amazingly, the only damage had resulted from the bumper's contact with a large boulder that had stopped its treacherous slide. Together, they had decided to leave the dent intact as an ongoing reminder of just how fragile life could be.

Now, as he stared at the same dent, that reality jolted Matt back to why he was here. He had texted Carol an hour ago, asking if they could talk. After a few short exchanges, they had decided to meet here at the parsonage. Where life, indeed very fragile he reminded himself, had been good for so long.

Inside he found her sitting in her recliner, an open photo album resting in her lap. After quietly taking a seat on the couch, he watched as she slowly turned its pages, tenderly caressing each one. She still wore the same jeans from Saturday but had swapped the orange tee shirt for a blue pullover blouse. Her hair, unwashed and straggly, was pulled back by a large bronze-colored clip that hugged the top of her head.

"She's so beautiful."

Is she talking about Angel? he wondered.

"She's too young to die."

Carol closed the album and sat quietly for a long minute. She looked at Matt. "She's made up her mind that she won't take any treatments, that in all her years of nursing, she's seen how little time they buy for a cancer like hers. Her doctor told her last week that without any it could be a matter of weeks."

"Does Brett know that?" Matt asked.

She nodded. "He overheard her tell me and left crying. I don't know where he is now." She paused reflectively. "Him being gone gave the two of us a chance to talk."

A loud gasp escaped her. "She told me over and over how sorry she was for betraying me. That it was all her fault and that you were not to blame. She asked me if I could forgive her. That she couldn't stand the thought of going to her grave not knowing I had." Her eyes snapped shut, her body shaking with grief. "I told her I forgave her. And then we hugged and cried together."

No longer able to hold it in, Matt spilled the question that had been burning inside him. "Do you think you can forgive me?"

"I thought it would be hard to forgive Linda," Carol said. "But it wasn't. When I thought about what she went through for all those years, I could see how she would fall for the attention another man might show her."

She held the album to her chest and stared mournfully at her husband. "Matt, I could sit here and say 'I forgive you' a hundred times. But in my heart, I wouldn't mean it. Not right now anyway. I need time."

She clutched the album tighter. Her tone stiffened. "It's different with you than with her. She was fragile that morning. You were not.

Being her pastor, and a married man, you should have stopped what was happening, could have stopped it, before it went too far."

She laid the album on the table next to her chair, then stood and walked to the opposite end of the couch and sat down. "Matt, it's not like I didn't show you the love and affection a wife is supposed to show her husband. I've got my faults. And that morning, I was upset. I was dealing with something I couldn't share with you. I know that didn't give me the right to leave here the way I did. But me being gone didn't give you the right to be unfaithful to me."

He had no rebuttal, no excuses. Every word she had said rang true in his heart. All he had to offer was assent. And a pledge to wait her out.

"I agree. Take all the time you need, Sweetness," he said softly. "I know I don't deserve it, but maybe someday, you can find a way to forgive me, too."

"However long Linda has, I have to be there for her, Matt. She's been like my sister all these years. She needs me. I know it'll be awkward, all three of us being together, but you need to be there for her, too."

For a long and tense minute, the two sat locked in a probing silence. Then, the air in the room lightened suddenly. Their gazes met. And what he saw in her eyes made him smile inside. The anguish that had been there just moments ago had now been replaced with an unmistakable longing.

For reconciliation, maybe?

She reached an outstretched hand toward him. As he took it in his, its warmth seemed to spread through his entire being.

Yes, he told himself, *there's hope.*

CHAPTER THIRTY-SIX

Tuesday, October 8th, 5:50 A.M.

An urgency blared forth from the familiar ring tone. At this wee hour, this wasn't just any call. He knew it was the one he had been dreading and expecting.

"Is she gone?" he asked.

"No," Carol answered feebly. "But it's getting bad fast, Matt. Really fast. You need to get over here now."

"I'll be there as soon as I can."

A month had passed since Linda had announced she was deathly ill. Since then, he had watched with anguish as the toxic beast slowly eating away at her had reduced her to little more than a shell. For days now, she had languished in bed, waiting the call from her Maker.

Brett had managed to juggle school and stay home with his mother. But for the past week, he hadn't left the house, spending every waking minute at her side. As much as he had longed to be there for his son, Matt had resisted, dropping in only occasionally for a few minutes at a time. In his heart, he knew these final days belonged to mother and son.

Carol had remained faithful to her best friend, tending her every need as along as she could. But over the past week, Linda's care had demanded more than she could handle, and hospice had been called in. And, like Brett, she had not left her friend's side, now holding

A Pastor's Story

vigil with him. Despite Linda's betrayal, the bond of sisterhood they had shared for two decades was now as strong as ever.

When Matt arrived at the house, Carol met him at the back door. Red-eyed from lack of sleep and her cheeks stained from constant crying, she looked ready to drop. Every ounce of him wanted to pull her to him, to comfort and console her. And his heart told him that's what she wanted. But he didn't push it, hoping the time would soon come when she would welcome his embrace,

"She told the hospice nurse to leave a little while ago," Carol said softly. "I think she knows she's about to go. She said she wants to talk to the three of us together." Her chin trembled.. "Prepare yourself, Matt. You're gonna be shocked at how she's gone down since the last time you were here."

When the two of them entered the bedroom, Matt caught his breath. Carol hadn't exaggerated. Linda lay propped upward by two satin pillows. Brett sat at her side holding her hand. Her eyes had sunk deep into their sockets. Her facial skin, pallid and sallow, was stretched so tightly over her cheekbones it looked like they would pop through at any minute. Under her gown, her lower abdomen was markedly distended, a stark contrast to the tiny waistline she had always managed to maintain.

"Come close to me," she said, motioning with her hand.

Carol walked to the side of the bed opposite Brett and sat down. Matt moved to the foot of the bed and stood.

"My time's come," Linda said matter-of-factly. "Before I go, I need to tell all of you some things. And ask you something, too."

With what strength she had left, she took Carol's hand in hers and locked fingers with both her and her son. She hesitated briefly, looking first in Brett's eyes and then into Carol's. Then, she raised her chin slightly and stared at Matt.

"You take care of these two, Matt," she said. "You owe it to them and to yourself."

She looked at Carol and smiled. "I guess I should tell you I'm sorry", she said, struggling to squeeze Carol's hand. Then, she looked at Brett. "But look at this fine young man we all got to raise together."

Carol choked back a rush of tears. "I'll take care of him. You know I will."

Linda exhaled loudly as the smile faded. "You're his mother now. And when I see Angel, I'll be her mother for you."

Carol couldn't hold back her tears any longer. "Give her a kiss for me. And tell her how much I love her and that I miss her so much."

Linda's upper body raised slightly. She gazed up as if longing for a glimpse of where she was headed. "I need all three of you to promise me something." She didn't wait for a response. "Promise me you'll be a family. Starting right now."

Brett leaned in and kissed his mother's cheek. "I promise," he whispered.

"I promise, too," Carol said, leaning forward to kiss her other cheek.

Linda looked at Matt expectantly. He raised his hands to his chest and pressed his palms together in a praying gesture. "I promise."

She smiled again. A look of peace settled over her face. Then, all at once, a prelude of calm filled the room. As Matt listened, there was complete and mortal silence except for the song of a sparrow somewhere outside the window, not far away. Seconds later, that

A Pastor's Story

sound melted away, replaced by a sudden elevation of Linda's breathing. He watched as her upper body rose and fell three times in rapid succession, before one final heave upward that lasted for several seconds.

Her eyes closed slowly. Then her chest reclined downward in one final breath.

CHAPTER THIRTY-SEVEN

Thursday, October 10th, 9:30 A.M.

Dawn had brought a fresh chill to the air and a fog that seemed to come out of nowhere. Shielded by low clouds, the grey mist hung over Memorial Gardens like a veil. As he drove along the south side of the narrow pathway that looped the graveyard on three sides, Matt could barely make out the three still figures gathered at the freshly dug grave site to the west of the large magnolia. He stopped at a point only feet from the tree's east branches and got out.

Before her death, Linda had insisted that there be no funeral. Her instructions to Carol had been short and direct: buy a cheap casket, bury me next to Bill, and move on. No ceremony to lament a life lost. No crowd of gossipers to offer false pity to those she left behind.

"Mom would have loved that shade of blue for her casket," Brett said as Matt walked up. He then pointed to the large spray on top of it. "And white carnations were her favorite."

Matt draped his arm around his son's shoulder. "Would you like some time alone with her?"

Brett wiped a tear from his cheek then nodded. With a jerk of his head, Matt motioned for Carol to join him as he walked away.

"I'll come back and close the grave this afternoon," Wendell said, turning to leave.

To Matt's surprise, Carol took his hand in hers as they walked toward Angela's grave. Her touch offered a welcome respite from the pall of the moment. And he couldn't help but hope that it was the beginning of something promising.

Since June, Angel's headstone had weathered a little more. The earth covering the grave was now even with that of the graves surrounding it. And although he had leveled the bench on his last visit, it once again sat tilted to one end. But there was one thing that hadn't changed: the brightness of Angel's smile beneath the oval glass that covered her face. It was as radiant as ever.

Carol released his hand and clasped her chin as a sigh of sadness escaped her. "This all seems so unfair. Can you figure any of it out?"

"I haven't yet. Not sure I ever will completely." He scratched an itch on the back of his head. "I figure you'll be staying at the house with Brett for the time being?'

"I promised Linda I'd stay with him at least for the rest of the school year. After graduation, he's not sure what his plans are."

She turned and gazed back toward the gravesite. "He's a strong young man." She looked at Matt. "We did a good job helpin' raise him."

"He's got a strong faith," Matt agreed. "He'll be fine with time."

The two of them stood quietly for a long, anxious minute. Finally, Matt broke the silence. "So where does this leave us, Carol? Do we have a future?"

She tiptoed and lightly pressed her lips to his cheek. "I can't answer that, Matt. I'm still sorting all this out. Right now, I think we just need to leave things as they are. Maybe after a few weeks, months even, we might have a clearer picture of where we are."

Matt pressed his finger to his jaw where she had just kissed him. "That tells me there's hope for us, Sweetness. I'm gonna hold on to that hope while I'm gone."

A frown creased her forehead. "Where are you going?"

"I sold Chuck's place yesterday to Jess McBay. He's bringing me a check this afternoon. Then, I'm headed outta town to the Eldridge Cabin."

Owned by longtime acquaintance and North Ward County native Homer Eldridge, the quaint, rustic cottage lay situated just north of where the Sabine River and Davis Creek merged, less than a mile from where Matt had grown up. On several weekends over the past two decades, he and Carol had retreated to the remote site for a quiet getaway. Yesterday, Matt had called Homer about using the cabin for a time of rest and reflection. His friend had offered it free for as long as Matt wanted it.

"How long will you be there?" Carol asked.

"As long as you need me to be." He reached into the pocket of his shirt. "Here. This should last you for a while," he said, handing her a folded check.

Upon opening it, her eyes widened. "Matt, I don't need $50,000.00 to live on," she said. "Linda had enough in the bank to last for several months. And Brett will be getting the proceeds of her life insurance. We'll be fine," she said assuredly, handing the check back to him.

Matt backed his hand away. "I insist you take it. Chuck would have wanted you to have part of what he left me. That still leaves over $100,000.00."

She tucked the check into the pocket of her slacks. Her gaze fell to Angela's picture. "Linda's hugged her by now. I know I'll see them both again someday, but knowing they're together makes me jealous. I hope my being a mother to Brett will take some of that jealousy away."

Matt draped his arm around her shoulder. And when she returned his embrace by circling his back, he drew her tightly to him. As if cued by the moment, rays of golden sunlight peeked through the grey clouds above them.

"Let's get back to our son," Matt said.

Again, they joined hands and walked slowly back to Linda's grave. By now the fog had lifted, revealing shadows beneath the stately magnolia. Brett drew the two of them into a hug. "Remember what we promised Mom before she died?" he asked.

"To be a family," Carol answered.

"That's right," Brett said. "Starting right now."

Carol shot Matt a firm look. "You need to tell him what you're about to do."

Brett stared expectantly at his father. "What's she talking about, Dad?"

"Son, I'm gonna be out of town for a while. Just to give your Aunt Carol some space...and time to think. About what the future holds."

"Where are you going?" Brett asked, his voice heavy with dismay.

"I'll be at the cabin on the river, up close to where I grew up. You'll have to drive up. Good bream fishing," Matt added hoping to soften his son's unease. "It's less than an hour away. And they just put up a new cell tower not far from there, so signal's good, I'm told. We can talk every day."

Brett looked at Carol. "Promise me something?"

"What, Sweetie?"

"Think fast. And figure this out quick so Dad can get back to us, okay?"

Carol smiled. "We'll see."

CHAPTER THIRTY-EIGHT

Thursday Afternoon, 12:30 P.M.

Baker Creek had slowed to a quiet crawl. As Matt tilted the large glass jar and poured its contents into the murky water, he could almost feel Chuck's presence hovering over this hallowed spot of ground. At his feet, the clump of ashes held together for a long minute before the gentle current pushed it toward the middle of the creek where it scattered before floating away.

Above the gentle rippling of the water, the sound of a slamming vehicle door sliced through the air. He screwed the lid back on the jar and tossed it into the water. It bobbed this way, then that before charting its own course downstream

"Goodbye, Buddy," he whispered.

Up the hill Jess McBay was waiting. A cattle rancher in his late forties, Jess was an imposing figure. Six-seven, big-boned, and broad-shouldered, he was known for his wide-brimmed straw hat, faded denim shirt, threadbare jeans, and pointed-toe cowboy boots. His brown hair descended his neck in a striking mullet that concealed his collar. A thick mustache and tapered goatee circled his lips. But it was his hands that defined him. From wrist to fingertip they were enormous, deeply tanned and calloused from hard labor.

"How are ya, Preacher?"

"Fair to middlin'," Matt replied. "Got a lot goin' on right now,"

Jess' smile relaxed. "I understand." His eyes panned from right to left. "This little piece of ground will square me up on the south side. And my hired hand's been livin' in a camper up the creek there. This house'll be just right for him."

Matt nodded. "That's good. I'm leavin' all the furniture inside. Most of it's old, but it's sturdy."

"He'll appreciate that," Jess said. "He don't have much. Where ya headed from here?"

"North. Up close to where I grew up." Matt's tone grew serious. "Carol needs some time to sort things out. I owe it to her to get out of the way for a while."

Jess stroked his goatee. "You're a good man, Matt. You did a lot for the church. I know I hadn't been real faithful as a member, but you were always there for me when I needed you,"

Matt grinned. "I appreciate that, Brother. More than you know."

Jess reached into his pocket and pulled out a check. "Thank you for the good deal you gave me."

"You're welcome," Matt replied. He stepped to his truck, reached through the open window, and grabbed a white envelope. He handed it to Jess. "Here's the deed."

"Shake on it, Preacher?" Jess asked, extending his hand.

As Matt had surmised, Jess' hand was strong and stiff, a testament to his physical vigor. But buried in that strength was a warmness that spoke to his gentle character.

Jess smiled and winked. "Good luck, Preacher."

"Thank you, Brother," Matt said as a sobering truth sank in. When the document Jess held in his hand went on record, he would officially be homeless.

Jerry swallowed hard and blinked away a tear. "I'm gonna miss you, Brother."

The two men stood outside the parsonage next to Matt's truck. It sat loaded, the bed filled with small furniture, the back seat packed with clothes and whatever else he had managed to fit into the space surrounding them. Carol's clothes and personal effects were at Linda's house. Everything else was packed away in Jerry's shop.

"I appreciate you storing the big stuff," Matt said. "Not sure how long you'll have to keep it." He shrugged. "Time will tell."

"You and Carol are gonna work this out," Jerry said firmly. "And quicker than you think," he added confidently.

Matt leaned against the truck. "Even if we do, I can't come back here, Jerry. I'd never be accepted here after what's happened." He paused, then posed the question he had long been wondering. "Do the church folks hate me?"

Jerry circled Matt's shoulder with his arm. "They don't hate you, Matt. They do feel betrayed. And disappointed that you didn't come clean a long time ago about what happened."

"I know I should have," Matt admitted. "But I'm human. Like everybody else. If I had confessed it, I knew in my heart what I'd lose. And how people would be hurt."

Jerry stepped in front of Matt to face him head on. "No matter what happened in the past, you'll always be my friend, Matt. I forgive you. And I know God's forgiven you, too." His eyes misted and a tear trickled from the corner of his eye. He pulled Matt to him, and they hugged tightly.

"I almost forgot," Matt said, reaching into his pocket. He backed away slightly and fished out the key to the parsonage. "I sure hope the next guy enjoys this place as much as I did."

A Pastor's Story

Jerry studied the key for a few heart-tugging seconds, then dropped it in his shirt pocket. "Promise me you'll stay in touch."

"You know I will," Matt assured him. "I love you, Jerry."

"I love you too, Pastor."

The two hugged again. After Jerry drove away out of sight, Matt climbed into his truck, started the engine, and sat. For five minutes... ten minutes...fifteen minutes. Finally, he pulled onto Oak Street, drove two blocks to 12th street, then turned left toward the four-way stop that led out of town. As he veered onto Highway 178 and headed north, he could almost feel an invisible door close behind him.

Five minutes later, Brett's ringtone echoed above the hum of the engine. "Hey, Son."

"Hi Dad. You left already?"

"Yep, I'm about ten miles out. What's up?"

A loud breath filtered into Matt's ear. "I just wanted to say 'I love you' and hope you can come home soon," Brett said. "And tell you I'll be up to see you in a few days."

"I'd like that, Son. Just let me know before you head my way."

"I will," Brett replied. "Aunt Carol wants to talk to you."

Matt braced himself. To his surprise, Carol's tone turned out to be soft and engaging.

"Matt, I wanted to ask a favor. Let's not talk or text for a week. I think that would be good for both of us. Don't you agree?"

Not really, he thought. But he knew he had to go along with her. "If that's what you think's best," he replied tongue-in-cheek.

"I do," she said. "We need to be apart at least that long with no contact. Maybe more. I'll text you a week from now if I need more time."

Matt felt his heart drop. "Sure," he said tersely.

"Did you want to talk to Brett again?"

"No. Just tell him I'll call him when I get settled in."

"I will. Bye, Matt."

He dropped the phone in the seat beside him. "A full week, maybe longer," he said out loud. It wasn't a long time. But it was a span of time he knew would plod by at a snail's pace. As his mind raced with the possibilities of all that could happen over the next seven days, an untimely but upbeat thought popped into his head.

The way he remembered it growing up, fishing on the Sabine River was at its best during the fall!

To Be Continued.